As the tail scythed towa
the ladder again. It travelled straight u
the tail smacked into it below the middle and flipped it over, the lower end arcing up and into the blinding whirl of the rotors. Matchwood was instantly everywhere, accompanied by a scream of protesting metal as the rotors shattered and the 'copter's engine accelerated to an impossible speed without their drag. The whole vehicle flopped heavily onto the edge of the roof and balanced momentarily before the counter-balancing torque of the tailblade swung it around with agonising slowness until the greater part of its weight hung in space over the street . . .

Dying Of Paradise

STEPHEN COUPER

SPHERE BOOKS LIMITED
30-32 Gray's Inn Road, London WC1X 8JL

Published in Great Britain by
Sphere Books Ltd 1982

DYING OF PARADISE is an original
publication containing some material from
THE LAST ROSE OF SUMMER © Stephen Gallagher 1978
published by Corgi Books

Set in Baskerville

Printed and bound in Great Britain by
Collins, Glasgow

1

The city had spread, over-reached itself and was beginning to die. There was little traffic, and the chattering of the helicopter carried clearly through the still air. The pilot was young, and flew with the arrogance of a newly-acquired but much-practised skill; he kept the 'copter below the roof level of the taller blocks and weaved a course between them. The swinging motion as the craft dipped to the left and right did nothing to temper Randall's inherent nervousness of flying and his knuckles grew white as they gripped the edge of the sealed Police Elite briefcase. The pilot was grinning, and every few seconds glanced across to see his reaction to the latest heartstopping manoeuvre. Randall's composure almost went as the side of a building raced to meet them and then shot past, seemingly only inches from the plastic bubble; windows zipped by in a stroboscopic blur and then they were out above the wide city again and flying level.

If the pilot felt a boyish disappointment, he didn't show it. Instead he tapped his combination microphone and headset and pointed behind the passenger seat. Randall forced his head to turn and saw a similar headset hanging ready for his use, so he reached for it one-handed, grunting slightly at the pressure of the restraining straps. Despite the microphone only an inch from his mouth, the pilot had to shout to be heard over the high-decibel clatter of the rotors.

'Sixty years old, this crate,' he said, taking his hand off the control column to gesture about the cramped cockpit. 'Oldest on the force. They can't afford to build any more.'

Randall nodded in what he hoped was an agreeable manner, but he felt his reserves of phlegmatic calm draining through a small hole somewhere deep inside. Fixing his eyes on the horizon he tried to imagine the solidity of concrete beneath him, but the unfulfilled wish only made his present agonies worse and he lapsed instead into contemplation of the unrolling cityscape. The pilot threw another glance and a grin, but at least he desisted from his hedge-hopping brinkmanship.

It was easy, at this height, to distinguish the dead wood from the merely diseased or dying. The tower blocks, their services long broken down and irreparable, were for the most part deserted, and on close passes it was possible to see past the reflection of the 'copter on the sightless windows into the gutted offices and apartments behind. However such views were so brief as to be dizzying; far easier on the eye were the sprawling developments of seven storeys and less which were slowly decaying in their brothers' shadows. Beyond the acres of citizens' housing was the glint of the river in the afternoon sun and beyond that, the underbelly, petering out into thin brown fields and the crumbling circles of the disused spaceport.

The 'copter jerked and bobbed suddenly as if on the end of an invisible leash; as it hung momentarily weightless it turned about its own centre and then roared into a dive towards the widening canyon of a broad city street. The pilot's grin remained but there were no sideways looks as he levelled off at two hundred feet and sped down the boulevard. The glass walls of the artificial valley's sides shot past in a blur of detail and it seemed to Randall that they were diving into a narrow shaft of infinite depth. Even through the headset the noise was far too loud as its battering was reflected back at them and as its pitch changed with each widening intersection, he felt a rolling followed by a minute correction as the change in airflow came and went.

Randall felt the tension ebbing away, his depths of fear and wonder finally explored and exhausted. He concentrated instead on the glittering reflection of the river which caught the sun and spilled up onto the windows at the far end of the canyon. The shimmering light seemed to spread and reach to envelop them at an impossible speed, then stars danced on the 'copter's bubble as they were out and climbing. The brief moment of weightlessness returned as they swivelled and dived into the final run, parallel to the water, towards the Police Elite main building. Randall found that his fingers were hurting from his grip on the briefcase and so he straightened them, one by one.

The great golden dome of Central Command lay before and below them, straddling the river. It shone in the afternoon light like a bright jewel amidst the dross of the city, dwarfing even the library annexe on its north side. Randall saw the 'copter's shadow rising to meet them as the ascending curve of the dome slid beneath and then the world tilted and the dome was gone.

Nose-up, the 'copter dropped towards its target, a white cross within a circle painted on the roof of the Police Elite building. They had to stand off for a little less than a minute whilst another 'copter lifted and circled from the same roof, and then they continued their downward progress to within a few feet of the asphalt surface.

Randall looked across at the pilot as he struggled to make a steady hover in a slight crosswind. 'Why aren't we landing?' He shouted into his microphone.

'Orders,' the pilot shouted back. 'This is as far as I can go. They say the roof's starting to give way.'

With an inward sigh, Randall replaced the headset in its clasp and undid his restraining straps. He had to steady himself as he attempted to rise and a gust drifted the 'copter close to the roof's edge; he glimpsed a thin sliver of eternity beneath the runners before the pilot made the necessary correction and coasted back to the centre of the circle.

The downdraught whipped at his hair and clothing as he opened the door in the bubble and leaned out. The height of the hover was varying between three and four feet - not a bad jump, but an uncertain one. He dropped and landed heavily, hearing the door slam closed behind him in the slipstream. As he regained his feet the 'copter was gone, and the hot wash of its exhaust across the roof was burning his eyes dry. Fighting the nervous tremble in his legs and disorientated by temporary deafness, Randall used his Detective's pass to call the elevator which would drop him to the approximate level of his office.

It was a hick planet in a dying system, under a star that burned too red for comfort. Generations before it had been a fast-developing new colony, but now it was nothing, struck off just about every trader's chart, too poor to matter – commercial suicide.

Of course, it hadn't always been that way. The time had been when Persephone's one habitable planet was the hottest commercial property in the known galaxy. It had been discovered by fluke; Tiny Carlisi, a shambling Spacer on Futures, Incorporated's exploratory vessel *Iron Star*, had been changing the ration packs in one of the ship's escape pods when he farted in free-fall. He was less interested in the consequent demonstration of Newtonian basics than in getting his orientation back, and as he flailed around helplessly the most accessible grip that fell under his hand was the panic handle. The iris lock slammed shut, and the pod was away.

There was some debate on the bridge about whether it would be worth getting him back. Tiny Carlisi's value as a human being never entered into it, because he had none; he was a Spacer, agile hands linked to a minimum of intellect and – at least in the major commercial vessels like the *Iron Star* – kept that way with drugs. The real argument over Tiny Carlisi hinged on the investment that he represented; was it worth the manpower and the delay to the mission to send somebody after him? But then, a trained spacer under full control was expensive to replace, and so Tiny Carlisi got rescued.

He wasn't difficult to track down. An escape pod operated under a simple directive, to find the nearest habitable body and get to it as fast as possible. The chase-up team found the only life-supporting planet within range, and then spotted Carlisi's beacon-blip. They found him sniffing flowers and floating two feet off the ground.

Not literally. They bundled him into the wingship and set off for the Iron Star with the pod in tow, and on the journey back he dug into his pockets and handed the crushed petals around. The rescue team had to be carried out at the other end, giggling and thoroughly plastered.

Discovery of the narcotic gave Futures, Incorporated a profitable new line. When they couldn't analyse, they colonised. The strange flowers couldn't be found anywhere else, and they couldn't be grown anywhere else; Futures therefore set its base under Persephone. Buildings went up fast, and they went up cheaply; upriver from a natural bay on the planet's one main landmass the major effort concentrated on a single city, a sprawling metropolis of traders and employees from the processing plants.

It took two hundred years to farm out the narcotic; two hundred years to harvest a plant so delicate that it resisted any attempt to rear it artificially. Two hundred years, and Persephone was commercially dead. The city by now held five million people; the investing companies looked around to see if they could dump this liability of human lives, and found that international law said they couldn't. Rapidly and with bad grace, they ploughed up the empty narc fields and seeded them with bacteria to produce a tolerable soil, planted the soil with a miserable selection of basic crops, and pulled out. They couldn't leave chaos, so they gave a couple of social engineers three weeks to come up with an answer. Three weeks wasn't long, but social engineers came expensive.

Their solution was rudimentary and offhand; no society's ever worked without being unfairly divided, they said. And that was it; not much to look at, but pretty damn good for three weeks of a social engineer's time. They turned it over to the Futures legal department, who expanded it slightly into twelve volumes of print.

The practical results were that all company employees were given citizen status, drawing a basic income from the agricultural turnover and the few remaining industries; everybody else had to manage, in accordance with the decree of unfair division. To make sure that it stayed that way, Futures left Central Command.

Fifty years later, the plans came up before the Trading States Commercial Court and were approved. The Court noted that a bare minimum had been accomplished in each of the required areas, but Futures hardly cared – they'd already moved on.

In a block that had once held the R & D labs, the *Festival of Futures* exhibition was still running; what once had been a state-of-the-art display was now a museum of antiquities.

Lee Rorvik stood by a window on the first floor. Some of the glass was split and some of it was missing; what remained was almost impossible to see through, but one of the gaps lined up with the roof of the Police Elite building several blocks beyond the opposite roofs. He watched as the 'copter began to climb. His eyes followed as it turned on its axis and slid into forward motion, and even after it had dipped beyond the roofline he watched until the chattering of its rotors could no longer be heard.

He knew he shouldn't be here. Not that it was a prohibited area – Central even listed it as an approved site – but he had obligations, an appointment. Even as he reminded himself, another part of his mind strained to push the thought away.

He was on the first floor gallery, one of the quieter sections. Most of the exhibits here were of the non-functional kind, no fun at all, and everybody tended to hurry through to the working exhibits – the light-up models of molecules, the speech-producing machines, the reader and tracker, and the cybernetics demonstrations. When he was much younger, dumped in the live-in baby farm by bored parents who found that Central's approval for breeding wasn't a passport to happiness, he'd visited the place a number of times; now it was noticeable that fewer of the exhibits were working. They broke and they failed, and they couldn't always be restored.

The museum was ungoverned and unattended, maintained by an enterprising group from the underbelly. They ran it under a thieves-kitchen arrangement; there were the guides who could run off a glib patter about any object and then look searchingly at you for a tip, and there were the self-taught technicians who ran little workshops in the old labs, rebuilding the re-jigging wherever they could to keep the *Festival of Futures* jogging along. One of the guides was crossing the gallery as Rorvik began to move away from the window; small, nervous and blond, almost an albino, he was keeping ahead of a group of citizen children, glancing back and grinning to make sure they were still with him. Following up the group was a baby-farm nanny, another underbelly. Rorvik felt a quiet twinge of inner contempt, and moved to follow them. They were heading in the opposite direction to the exit. It was enough.

The nanny was carrying a glowing static rod. Wherever she waved it, the group shrank back in a tide. It flowed without noise or effort around the guide as he stood by something that looked – to Rorvik at least – like a new piece. Some of the serious little faces turned to him as he demonstrated; others turned anywhere else, listless and inattentive.

It was a gram machine, nothing more. Probably not even part of the original exhibition, it had more likely been looted from some sealed-off part of the city by an underbelly raiding party sneaking back across the river at night. The music was godawful, the rhythm half-buried and too many sounds to sort out. The nanny tipped the guide to dismiss him, and then swept the party onward. When the children didn't move fast enough for her, she touched about with the static rod; there were flashes and cracks and yelps, but no tears. Citizens had nothing to cry about. Citizens were Central's chosen.

Watching them go, Rorvik realised too late that he was alone with the guide.

'Bet you've never seen one of these before, have you?' the guide said, stroking the case of the gram, and though he'd seen plenty Rorvik uneasily admitted that he hadn't.

'I know you'd like to hear it.' The guide took a step forward and Rorvik took an involuntary step back; the underbelly was simply moving around to the other side of the machine, and he looked up with a wide, flat smile that on the surface said *friend* but which echoed to the depths with contempt; the natural friction of unsympathetic opposites.

Rorvik had already heard it, and hadn't liked it much. He nodded. 'Sure I would.'

He'd pulled the trap closed around himself. There was some crude welding on the side of the case, a rough-cut slot for coins with a little box of mechanism underneath. The visitor must provide, and so Rorvik had to dig in his pocket for the small handful of change that he usually carried in addition to his Central credit card.

He knew he was being duped, that the box on the side contained nothing more than a few drops and levers to make clicking noises before the guide reached around behind the machine to restore power, but he played along and pretended to look interested. It was no better the second time around. The whole idea was a waste, a dead end; if you needed music Central provided it better, piped straight to every room of your apartment. It changed with the light, with the seasons, with the weather; it was always appropriate and it never jarred. Unlike the gram, which would need effort and attention – okay for the underbelly, perhaps, but citizens were used to the real thing.

After feigning attention for a while, he dug in his pocket again. He overtipped, and then when he realised it tried to pretend that it was normal for him; the underbelly grinned and nodded, not giving any thanks.

He started to move towards the exit. Some of the other

guides tried to attract his attention but he shook his head briefly and moved on, knowing that if he hesitated he'd never be able to disengage himself.

He made it to the outside without being drawn into conversation. Most of the guides would drop an unwilling mark and move onto the next, more likely prospect; only a few would block and divert and whine until they got what they wanted, but fortunately none of these got in his way.

Rorvik was halfway down the steps at the front of the building before he allowed himself to slow down and look around. The boulevard was wide and its surface was cracked after long disuse, and most of the buildings along it were blind and shuttered. Over on the far side, two old women were pushing a handcart loaded with rags; a few underbelly children followed at a distance, watching the nondescript novelty. If they didn't get back over to the other side of the river before the curfew barriers went up they'd probably be spending the night in the damp and dark of some badly-sealed city cellar, and maybe by morning the crawlers would have had them. They shuffled along, dark-eyed and skinny; one girl had no shoes, her feet bound in flapping rags.

There was a noise, off down the boulevard. Over a mile away another Police Elite helicopter dropped in between the buildings and began the bravado run at top speed down the canyon. There was no navigational justification for the route but nearly all the pilots followed it, skimming the tops of the thin dead trees and making them bend and lose a few leaves every time. Nobody could tell them to stop, for the pilots were an élite within an élite and did much as they pleased. They manufactured more excitement for themselves in one afternoon than a citizen could hope to get in a whole lifetime of hobbies and diversions.

The 'copter roared up and was gone in an instant, diving towards the river like a plummeting stone. Rorvik had caught a brief flash of the tableau within the 'copter's bubble; the pilot straining forward and grinning like a demon, his passenger frozen in an attitude of disbelief. He had watched the run so many times, envied its daring and feared its risks, and now he waited for the swooping climb across the water, invariably delayed until the last possible moment and then bursting up into the air like an explosion of joy.

The pilot was in trouble. Impossible to see why, but the tail of the 'copter was swinging from side to side so that the machine repeatedly tilted and dipped in its headlong progress down the man-made ravine. It was almost too late when the pilot regained a measure of control; the crevasse opened out and the stunted trees of the riverside rushed at his runners as the 'copter's nose came up, up and cleared them; and then continued to rise, impossibly fast as the pilot fought the controls to follow through and soar out over the open river where a dignified ditching might at least be possible.

The flickering tailblades fouled in the uppermost branches, and the rising nose was thrown up and over. The 'copter somersaulted lazily, and as it reached the apex of its loop the whirling blades suddenly regained their bite on the air and slammed all the machinery down hard in the middle of the road. In the same instant fuel spurted and burned, and a cloud of black fire mushroomed out in all directions.

A moment of surprising quiet was cut by a second explosion which sent a rainbow of burning fuel high into the air. It settled to the angry whisper of distant fire and then, leaking from the building behind Rorvik, the insipid background music programmed by Central Command.

The fuel was still showering, the light-show continued. Now that, thought Rorvik, is what I *call* an exhibition.

Rorvik's appointment was with a set of empty rooms. Because Jiri Mondrian wouldn't be in them, they would be strangers; Jiri Mondrian would probably never be going home again. His woman had packed up and cleared out some time before, and Jiri's place had been ideal for getting together in the long afternoons that stretched into the lonely evenings, all three of them – Rorvik, Jiri, and Lin Baxter.

He climbed moving walkways that no longer moved, through empty shopping malls with kicked-in windows – flyblown and crumbling by day, this was no place to be seen at night. Through a gap across a piazza he glimpsed the far-off dome of Central Command. It gave him a guilty start; he'd missed out on the library facility for several months, and he felt that perhaps he should get along there for the sake of appearance if nothing else.

But he couldn't raise any enthusiasm for the soap operas and space adventures, not since he'd found that he was able to join in with the dialogue and get it right most of the time. On his last visit to the library he'd been given a gentle reprimand for his neglect of the citizens' greatest privilege, and the prospect of facing yet again that blank console in the curtained booth and hearing displeasure in the fatherly voice of Central Command did little to entice him. Louann would be there, of course, collecting her usual armful of sloppy dramas, and perhaps that would be family representation enough.

He let himself in with Jiri's key. It was a standard-issue place, two small bedrooms and a smaller kitchen packed in an *L* around the main lounge, four of these units to each level with a central service well – it wasn't much different to his own. The suitcase that Jiri had asked for was easy to find; vacuum-formed and with one broken hinge, it contained everything that Jiri owned.

Rorvik was embarrassed to be seen with it, and ashamed to be embarrassed. It was a lousy way to feel about somebody who was dying.

His shoulders were aching with the effort of carrying when he finally arrived back at his own apartment block and managed awkwardly to jab the *Call Lift* button with his elbow.

There was a blast of badly-tuned radio programming

from the other side of the hall. Collinson, the block caretaker, had opened the door to his little glassed-in office and was shaking his head as he leaned out.

'The lift's burned out on us again,' he said. 'It'll have to be the stairs until we get the requisition to have it fixed.' Collinson was underbelly, but like all city employees he had a dispensation from Central to live on the citizen side of the river.

Rorvik groaned inwardly and debated whether to leave the suitcase in Collinson's office and collect it when the lift was working again, but that would be a week at least on the past performance of Central's maintenance units. They were underbelly too, after all. He thanked the caretaker - no tip, so tough luck - who nodded and withdrew into his hutch.

It was five floors, and the suitcase got heavier at every turn in the stairs. The fourth floor was old Gerrard's level, and he started to tiptoe on the creaking treads before he realised that there was enough noise coming from Gerrard's place to drown out an avalanche of ball-bearings in the stairwell. It was a relief - if Gerrard knew you were passing, he'd be out and launched into a conversation which needed nothing from you beyond your presence. So he was old and lonely - he was also a pain, and impossible to get away from.

He emerged onto the fifth level and dropped the luggage on the grimy hall carpet. It saved him the trouble of having to hunt one-handed for his key; he pressed it against the lock panel where the circuits conformed and released the door.

Louann wasn't home. Probably the library, as he'd thought; there was a sense of disturbance, of something misplaced, but nothing more. Citizen liaisons didn't last, and they weren't encouraged; they should have broken two years before, when the real bitterness had been at its height - the coldness that followed had been far worse, made perfect hell by the numbness of routine. One of them should have moved out, but the steady deterioration of the housing blocks meant that there was nowhere to go; even Jiri's place was already spoken for and due for occupation.

The three-screen video was dark in the corner, and he went over to it and placed his hand on the control surface. Still warm. She couldn't have been away for long.

Jiri hadn't given any instructions on what to do with the contents of the case. There was only one item that he'd asked for, and that was on top when the lid came up; half a bottle of bootleg hooch, real varnish-stripper. As for the rest, Rorvik was supposed to be storing it – not that Jiri would ever see it again.

The rest of the contents was junk, there was no kinder way of putting it; old junk, the kind that has no worth but which gives you a few minutes of interest and the odd flash of warmth sorting through. Rorvik lifted a few things out, turned them over, moved others aside; Jiri seemed to have stayed with his parents for longer than standard, and even to have been sent letter cassettes at the baby farm. Rorvik didn't even know where his own parents lived.

There was a knock on the door – he hadn't locked it behind him. He reached to pull the suitcase lid down as a wary head was thrust into the room, closely followed by the rest of Lin Baxter.

'Guess who,' he said, and then looked around with hard interest. There were a couple of Library cassettes in his hand, the video/sound type. Anywhere but on Persephone they would have been curious antiques, but on the burned-out narcotic world progress had hit the skids when Futures moved out. 'Where's Louann?' he demanded. 'You been keeping her hot for me?'

Rorvik put on a smile that barely fitted, and hoped the cracks didn't show. 'She's down by the docks, corrupting the fleet,' he said. 'But I can put you down for an evening appointment.'

'Any time,' Baxter said airily. 'I know you find it tough to keep up the energy. Do you some good to let an expert in.' He closed the door and came into the room. Lin Baxter lived alone after a string of no-go liaisons, at least three as far as Rorvik knew. Two of the girls had been more than ordinarily engaging; a surface gloss of happiness had masked hidden distances that had proved, in the end, uncrossable. They broke without acrimony, more with bafflement. Baxter's explanation, thrown out with bitterness in his darker moments, was a simple one. He didn't think that he could hope to love anybody else more than he loved himself.

His eyes were on the case. His expression was mildly troubled, as if something was worrying him - but he wasn't sure what. 'I'm going down to Central,' he said. 'Feel like a walk?'

'I'm staying clear of Central,' Rorvik said as he lifted the case and carried it over to the lay-low. 'I've left it too long. I can't face the questions.'

'Oh fuck,' Baxter said suddenly as the pieces clicked together. 'That's Jiri's, isn't it?'

Rorvik nodded. Baxter had gone slightly pale, drained of ease. He couldn't handle it; a dying friend got under his defences, and his shell was too thin to take it.

'I'm going out again,' Rorvik said, lifting the lid on the junk. 'Will you come with me?'

Baxter slowly shook his head. His eyes were still on the case, portable museum and reminder of transience. Everything that Jiri Mondrian owned; worthless junk, and now a body to match.

'I can't,' he said. 'I can't.'

Rorvik felt a glow of anger, but it was wrapped in guilt. So he made the trips and he sat with Jiri, but deep down his feelings were little different from Baxter's, an inexplicable mixture of shame, impatience and despair. Duty sent him out to the wards on the fringe of the city; real friendship would have kept him away from the deteriorating spectacle of a wasting life.

'Okay,' he said, making it light in an effort to break the mood, 'I'll take a walk down to the river with you. But I'll stay clear of the Library.' The Central Computer's cool disapproval was something he didn't need. The real advantage lay in the fact that he'd be out of the apartment when Louann got home.

He moved to close the case, but Baxter moved first. He'd seen something, and he reached for it.

A rotten elastic band ripped and spilled the plastic slips of a dozen or more photographs. Age had defocussed the stereo images, blurs that hung like a mist before long-dead faces. Baxter wasn't after these, but something underneath; he pushed them aside, and then tugged out a cassette.

'Look at this,' he said. It seemed a real museum piece, sound only with no vision track and a faint bloom which killed the shine on the plastic case. It wasn't even a standard Library coded colour. 'I wouldn't return it There's probably fifty years of fines backed up on it.'

'I doubt it,' Rorvik said, taking the cassette from him and turning it over. 'This isn't a Library tape.'

Baxter looked blank, and Rorvik turned the cassette around to show him the back. There was no Library seal, no customary embossed warning about the illegality of attempting to open or copy the cassette, and no list of penalties involved if it should be found in the hands of any non-citizen.

'Not a Library tape?' Baxter said. 'It can't be pre-Library. They were all collected and destroyed.'

'It must be underbelly, then.'

'Underbelly?' Baxter blinked, and grew slightly nervous. 'What do you mean?'

'Nobody in the underbelly is supposed to get access to Library stuff, but it's known that they make their own gear. This probably fits some lash-up machine.'

'Better get rid of it, then.'

'Don't you want to hear it?'

'No. Get rid of it.' Baxter's growing fear was obviously real. No citizen treated a Central ban lightly.

Rorvik looked at the cassette again. It seemed innocent and homely, probably knocked up in an antique vacuum-forming plant in some shady underbelly cellar on the far side of the river. It probably wasn't pornography – not without a video track – and Rorvik was intrigued by what it might be. Perhaps a ripoff dub of some Central programming, or maybe something a little more unusual. He'd try to find out.

Baxter followed him across the room as he went towards the video. 'You can't play it,' he said. 'It won't fit.'

'It might.' The cassette was slightly smaller than standard, but the tape pitch looked about the same. As long as the drive cores engaged and the band was against the heads, the air-pressure positioning and laser alignment would handle the rest. He reached to slot it in, and Baxter's hand closed on his wrist.

He pulled it back again immediately, almost apologetically. 'Please,' he said. 'Please, don't try to play it.'

Rorvik looked at him, more surprised than anything. 'Aren't you even curious?' he said.

'No. Don't play it.'

He found it difficult to understand Baxter's apprehension. No citizen messed around with infringements if he wanted to *stay* a citizen, but surely here, an action that would be unobserved and of no particular consequence . . .

'What's the matter?' he said. 'What's the scare?'

'Central, that's the scare. What if Central's monitoring?'

Central Command took occasional samples of feedback from the videos, charting times and incidence of use and planning its citizen administration programme accordingly. 'The chances are pretty thin. And even so, Central only takes a power sample. It wouldn't know what we were playing.'

'What *you* were playing. Keep me out of this.'

Baxter was really scared, as if Rorvik had just proposed that it would be a great joke to sneak downstairs and strangle old Gerrard as he sat blotting out his misery with Squeeze and muzak. Respect for authority was bred into every citizen, but Baxter seemed to have a respect that had over-developed into a phobia of disobedience. It was a facet of Baxter that Rorvik had never really seen before. He wasn't sure that he liked it much.

'Look,' he said. 'It's a tape, that's all. It can't frighten anyone and it can't hurt anyone, and I'd be interested to hear it. I don't see what logical objection Central could have.'

'We're not talking about logical objections. We're talking about rules.'

'Rules are fine for out there. But this is my own home.' He was aware of a kind of sick irony in the words as he said them in the bare, charmless suite of rooms that had been systematically cleaned out of warmth and affection during the last couple of years. Baxter looked around, not so much searching for the truth of Rorvik's assertion as for a means of escape should the Police Elite suddenly come hammering on the door. The efficiency of Central's executive was legendary; the railed fire escape that he could see through the window of the open bedroom would probably be no salvation at all.

'Either stay or go,' Rorvik said, 'but here it comes.' He pushed the cassette into the slot, which flipped open to accept it.

'Probably won't work,' Baxter said hopefully.

Louann Roget was still two hundred yards from the entrance as she approached the Library, but she was already in the shadow thrown by Central Command's dome in the afternoon sun. She joined the short queue at the turnstiles and quickly passed through the security procedure into the main hall. It was wide and low-ceilinged, not unlike the disused passenger lounges at the old spaceport, but the visual impression barely registered with her; she followed a familiar route across half an acre of floor to the broad steps which led to the mezzanine and the fiction terminals.

The mezzanine was far more crowded than the main floor level. Citizens of all ages but of the same basic appearance passed before and behind her with armloads of tapes identical to her own. In spite of the crowd she had little trouble finding a vacant booth. She sat down, sliding the door closed behind her, and the echo and shuffle of the broad hall was lost in the stuffy acoustic of the booth's interior.

It was narrow – a minimum space – but comfortable. A low hum seeming to come from nowhere and everywhere at the same time denoted that the Central Command computer was aware of her presence, and the mirror directly opposite her at eye level thinned and became transparent to reveal the glow of a single camera eye.

'Good afternoon, and welcome to the Library facility of Central Command.' Again, the voice seemed to surround and contain her. It was deep and well-modulated, with a tone that was paternal and affectionate. 'Please place your borrower's card in the slot in front of you and state your name. Remember that to give a false identification is an offence.'

'Louann Roget.'

'You are identified, Ms Roget. Good afternoon.'

'Good afternoon.' She retrieved her borrower's card from the slot.

'And what can the Library do for you, Ms Roget?'

'I've come to return these tapes and to get some new ones.'

'Please place your tapes in the delivery chute on your left.' On cue, a flap popped open with a hiss of compressed air and she obediently slotted the cassettes into it. The lid smacked closed again and a soft whoosh was evidence that the computer was using a vacuum chamber to suck at a loop of tape from each in turn and give it a spot-check.

'Ah,' the voice said, 'three dramas and a hobby tape. Tell me, Ms Roget, how did you enjoy "The Shivering Willows?" '

'Very much, thank you.'

'We find it is one of our most popular choices. So moving. I shall note your remarks for future recommendation.'

'I watched it twice.'

'So I see. Please remember to rewind the tape next time, Ms Roget.'

She gave a guilty start. 'Oh ... I'm sorry.'

'Please don't worry about it, Ms Roget. Just make sure you rewind all the tapes next time. Now, what else did we have? I see you borrowed "Arabic Passion" for the second time.'

'If you remember, you suggested it to me.'

'Of course I remember, Ms Roget. We never forget anything. How is Lee Rorvik?' The tone of the voice remained the same as it effortlessly switched subjects.

'Quite well, I suppose. We don't often talk.'

'So you said last time. Where is he now?'

'He was out somewhere when I left the flat. I've no idea what he was doing.' Her eyes were fixed on the chute where her new selections would be delivered, and she began to wish as she did on every visit that the computer would cut short the friendly conversation.

'How much did you enjoy "Gangster's Moll"?'

She warmed at the memory. 'Quite a lot. I've always liked historical romances.'

'He hasn't been into the Library for three months now.'

'I'm sorry?'

'Lee Rorvik. I was wondering why he had not visited us recently.'

Now she began to grow impatient, but knew she dared not show it. Instead she stared longingly at the empty chute, and replied without much enthusiasm, 'I wouldn't know. He spends most of his time with a couple of his friends.'

'Names?'

'Lin Baxter's one of them. The other one's called Jiri Mondrian, but he's sick. Out at the spaceport wards.'

'May I suggest some new tapes for your enjoyment.' A hiss of air announced the welcome arrival of a cassette in the chute. 'Here is "Her Heart on Her Sleeve", a tender drama set in the world of retail management. I'm sure you'll find it very illuminating.'

'I'm sure I will.'

'Where does Baxter live?' This time, the sudden switch caught her slightly off-guard.

'Citizen block twelve,' she faltered. 'Across the street from our block.'

'Here is your second selection. It is called "Susan of the Steelworks". What does Baxter do?'

'I wouldn't know. I don't like him.' Louann removed the cassette and looked eagerly for the next.

'I see. This is "Her Trust Rewarded, a Romantic Tale of Old Tyneside". That was it. She had what she needed, and the rest would be just tiresome social set-dressing.

'Thank you,' she said.

'Ask Lee Rorvik to call on us more often,' the voice purred. 'We would hate to see him fall idle.'

'He seems to find plenty to occupy himself.'

'I am sure he must. Unfortunately, such occupations can so often turn out to be of a disagreeable nature. Ask him to call on us.'

'I will.'

'Tell him we have new material to interest him. Tell him we remember his tastes, we remember his appetites. Tell him we never forget ... anything.'

'I'll tell him.'

The voice of Central Command became more business-like. 'Please take your final selection from the delivery chute on your right. The Library division of Central Command thanks you for your visit, Ms Roget. We look forward to your return.'

The hum subsided, and the light died in the camera eye. She was left facing her own reflection in the mirror, and the noise of the world outside began to penetrate the door.

New tapes. Three whole days of bliss in the best of all possible worlds. She slid the door open and hurried out across the mezzanine.

The cassette hadn't wanted to fit at first; it was too narrow, and although it was possible to get the tape up against the heads the casing was at too much of an angle. Rorvik jammed a stack of canteen coupons underneath to hold it firm; otherwise, the tape would have snarled as soon as the machine began to draw it out.

He programmed in the threading operation. As power was cycled into the now-cold apparatus a small panel lit which read, 'machine not ready'. They both waited for it to blink out.

'I'm mad,' Baxter said mournfully. 'I shouldn't even *be* here.' But he made no move to go. After a moment, he said, 'What do you think it is?'

'Why so curious?' Rorvik said. 'I thought you were ready to jump out of the window, just to get away from it.'

Baxter shrugged. The warning panel went abruptly blank, and then flashed a 'ready' light. As Rorvik reached for the playback control Baxter gave an involuntary glance towards the windows and the iron stairs. No Elite were gathering outside, nobody was getting ready to kick his way in. And there was no sound coming from the video. 'What's wrong?' he said. Underneath the apprehension was an ill-disguised sliver of disappointment.

'Not sure,' Rorvik replied, and he moved the cassette around slightly in case it hadn't engaged. 'It's so old and non-standard there might not be a guide track. I don't know.'

'Perhaps there's ... ' Baxter began, and the music started.

At first, it was disappointing. It was like Classico, the best stuff that Central reserved for late nights and serene summer days, but it wasn't half as easy to listen to. There was no real regular beat – or rather, it was there by implication only, as if one of the tracks had been erased in the final mix. The melody wasn't something you could whistle; not really a melody at all, because it didn't repeat to force its way home and give instant, easy familiarity.

Baxter was frowning and shaking his head. 'Crap,' he said. 'Better knock it off.'

'Give it a chance,' Rorvik argued. He agreed with

Baxter, but form demanded that he should be the one to pick the moment when he pressed the tape cancel.

And suddenly, he was there. It was an unperceived jump, a gestalt leap where the pieces dropped together in an unforced whole; he didn't listen to the music, he was within it, dazzled and slightly giddy like a man in a world of blacks and whites getting his first sight of blood. The last unit which made the gestalt complete was the listener, Rorvik He was part of a chain of understanding which led back to the music's raw source; a source which, though inexplicit and obscure, was traceable through the clues of personality contained in the sound.

You didn't get clues of personality in Central's output. That was the shaker, the three-star shocker, pay your money and step up to see the freak show. Some*body* had put all this together.

Baxter hadn't seen it. His face was still the same composed blank that it had been at the start of the cassette, with now an obvious shadow of boredom sneaking in. And now, Rorvik realised, his own understanding was starting to slip; he'd had one intense moment of imprint, and conscious effort couldn't hold it as it started to fade.

The door opened, and Louann stepped in from the hall.

Baxter was on his feet straight away, before he'd even seen who was coming. Rorvik was looking up as Louann closed the door behind her and then turned into the room. She was frowning as she looked towards the singing video with its dead screens.

'Were you listening to that?' she said, carefully phrasing in order to demand a polite negative. There was a pained edge to her voice which made the effect complete.

'No,' Baxter said quickly, and when he saw that Rorvik wasn't going to move he leaned across to the *stop/eject* control. He whisked the cassette out and away behind his back before Louann could see that it was non-standard. Two coupons fell to the floor.

'I'd better be going,' he said as he backed around Louann and towards the door. 'Regards to Jiri, and tell him . . . ' Baxter's voice tailed off as he realised that he had nothing to say to Jiri. But by then, he was nearly away. 'Well, anyway, regards to Jiri.' The smiling mask with fear in its eyes was starting to slide as he pulled the door closed.

Louann was indifferent to Baxter's leaving, and she didn't show any sign of curiosity at the sounds that she'd heard or the odd container that she may or may not have glimpsed. She set her own stack of cassettes down by the video, and picked one off the top. 'Central was asking about you,' she said.

Rorvik looked up. 'About me?'

'Your attendance record. Central's getting worried about you.'

At least somebody *is*, he thought, and then he thought of Jiri, alone and unwanted in a grim ward in the spaceport. This is where we're all headed. This is the real measure of Central's concern.

The three wraparound screens flared into life with an aerial view descending on an industrial complex. *We present, 'Susan of the Steelworks'*, boomed the speakers, *'a tale of soaring passion in the rolling mills. Come back with us now to a time when men were men and women were worshipped, for a tale of a tragic prisoner of love . . .'*

Lin Baxter had nothing but a long series of bad moments as he made his way down the stairs and out of the building, past Collinson's noisy little office. Although he'd hidden the non-standard cassette between his own Library issues, it seemed to sing in a loud and piping voice: '*Guilty, guiltee*!' it shrieked happily at anyone it passed, but only Baxter could hear the song.

Forget the Library for this afternoon. Wait until dark, and then go down to the river. Find a heavy stone and bind the cassette to it, choke off its song forever in the fast-moving waters. Throw it high and hard, over towards the underbelly.

Send it back to its own.

2

Rorvik loitered around the street near the museum for almost a week. The Police Elite helicopter pilots no longer made the bravado run down the enclosed roadway to the river. The previous week's crash obviously made them wary. One of them had hovered for a while at the far end of the steet like a thoughtful wasp, and Rorvik had watched it hopefully; but it swung up and away on a safer route across the rooftops, and he was disappointed. On one morning he actually went back into the museum and looked again at the gram deck, but there was no satisfaction in it.

Twice he even followed the street down to the river and looked speculatively across at Central Command. Seen this close, the dome showed itself not to be a simple orb but a geodesic structure, the great sweep of its curve being formed by a mass of jointed triangular plates which glittered in the cold sunlight like the facets of a diamond. There, he thought, is where I should be looking; Central Command was, after all, the sole source of all music and entertainment, and anything remotely musical must have its origins there.

But Rorvik doubted it. He had never been an avid Library user, but he knew the range of the stocks well enough to recognise that Jiri's old tape had a content so unlike anything he had ever heard before that it might well be from off-planet. That possibility depressed him intensely; the city's spaceport was long decayed, and the commerce of the galaxy had been bypassing them for more than a generation now. It would be a week or more before he could amass enough credit actually to take the monorail to the thin, reedy green belt where the nursing homes clustered, and until then he could only walk the streets and watch for helicopters.

There were, of course, other reasons for avoiding Central Command - or rather, the Library division, as nobody ever went beyond its halls and terminals into the machine habitat of the dome. Baxter was to a great extent correct in his apprehension towards security action over a communications infringement. Rorvik couldn't be certain that the very act of listening to the old-time music might not be construed as an offence, and to admit so much would invite an inevitable chain of questions revealing the existence of the tape and his use of an unofficial cassette. When the Library knew *that*, he could wave goodbye to his citizenship and all its benefits. Home, food and income would vanish in a flash, his credit would be blocked and he would never again have access to the Library - although of all the penalties, that one troubled him least.

The range of possibilities outside an enquiry to Central Command were so small as to be negligible. Nearly everything could be tracked back to the Central computer, sitting in its private dome like a great immobile hermit crab, sifting, comparing and issuing decisions on every subject from sewage flow to housing. If Rorvik by some indiscretion were to allow a suspicious action to come to its attention it would be a matter of moments before the relevant programmes were meshed and correlated to send the Police Elite hammering on his door.

No. Direct appeal to the computer was out of the question. He was both dejected and frustrated; it was such a *small* thing to ask, such a ridiculous issue to be fearful over, but he was certain of the unevitable consequences. He left the river and wandered down towards the commercial sector.

The drab fronts of the markets held little attraction for him, but as the day drifted on into early evening their brightly-lit interiors in contrast with the dark pearl of the sky gave each the false aura of a centre of excitement.

There was nothing he wanted, and nothing he could afford if he were to be making the monorail trip next week, but it cost nothing to look. Others were looking also, mainly non-citizens, lingering with dreams in their eyes.

The thought struck Rorvik as he passed the third frontage. As he had crossed each open doorway the sweet gentleness of the background music had washed around him and receded as he moved on, only to find himself in the cross-current from the next opening. He stopped abruptly, and earned a growl from a man following head-down and a little way behind. Rorvik mumbled something that would sound like an apology as they shuffled around each other. The other man said nothing, and didn't even look at him.

There were plenty of deep shelves inside, angular and mostly empty in the hangar lighting. Although citizens used such places, they didn't use them often; they were mainly for the underbelly who worked within the city's limits and couldn't use the citizen facilities. Stock control was by Central, of course; after a while you would get used to the irregular stock dates, the sudden gluts, and the immediate sellouts which kept the underbelly nervous and undersupplied, an urban peasantry.

Rorvik stepped inside. At first, nobody noticed him. The muzak cut out abruptly and the air thundered as somebody blew into a microphone.

'Good evening, shoppers,' a voice came over with poorly-feigned cheer. 'We would like to draw your attention to some of the bargains of the food section, where textured protein is now selling at four credits below the recommended price. Swedes are also down in price today, so why not treat the family to something special this weekend?'

It was a man with dark, slicked-down hair and heavy glasses who could be seen in a partitioned office raised above floor level at the back of the store. 'Moving on to our cosmetics counter, for a limited period we are offering free medical insurance to every buyer of our "Wrinkle Killer" home facelift preparation. Remember, shoppers, this is your big bargain store where your credit's worth more.'

Rorvik called out 'Excuse me!' and walked towards a figure in a white coat bending over a pile of food bags. It turned out to be a youth of little charm and great personal odour.

'You talking to me?' he said, almost as if reacting to an accusation.

Rorvik was nonplussed, and said 'I was, actually, yes.'

'What do you want?' the youth demanded.

'Piece of information.'

The youth jerked his thumb in the general direction of the raised office. 'Information point's over there.'

Now Rorvik was getting a problem. The cassette had been underbelly, a bootleg; how could he say, openly, that this was what he was looking for?

He moved a little closer. The smell was like bad meat being stewed in turpentine. An information point would be a terminal with a readout of current stock levels and prices; 'I don't want to talk to the machine,' he said. 'I want something more unofficial.'

The youth nodded slowly. He looked much older, close up. He said, 'Like what?'

Clandestine behaviour had never been familiar to him, outside of the show tapes where it was sketched in parody; the good guys always had the upper hand, and the scum showed a suitable deference and respect. Rorvik didn't feel much like a good guy; just way out of his depth. 'Like . . . like music,' he said.

It didn't seem possible, but the youth got slightly uglier. 'You pissing me about?' he demanded, and when Rorvik shook his head he went on, 'I can get you meat and I can get you book-filth, but it would cost you. You want music, fuck off down to your Library.'

'I've seen a tape cassette,' Rorvik insisted as the youth tried to walk away. 'It was underbelly, I know it. I want to know where I can get more.'

'Talk to Morden,' the youth spat, 'if you can find him.'

And then he started to laugh as he turned and walked off.

Big fleas have little fleas; for every market there's a fleamarket, a passing-place for junk as it sifts down through the social layers to the poorest and hungriest at the very bottom. That meant underbelly, and so the fleamarket shops on the fringe of the commercial sector were where Rorvik went to look next.

They were in the lowest part of the city's shopping mall, an area originally set out for land vehicle parking. Now the only land vehicles belonged to the Elite and to some of Central's maintenance departments, and the levels had been colonised. Halfway between bazaar and graveyard, the bays had been walled off into deep chambers and lights had been strung from the mall's main power supply. It was a rats' nest of a market, long snaking alleyways and a concrete sky with neon stars. Those who couldn't pay the controlling gangs for a unit kept stalls in the alleys, and the very lowest spread out on rugs under the stalls. Such a place ought to be busy, noisy, shrill with hustling. It was almost silent.

Nobody called out to him as he wandered; he was citizen, and to be avoided even if his money wasn't. He chose his place - well, not really carefully. He tried to exercise some judgement, but in the end he chose at random. It was a deep bay with shutters drawn back, mostly filled with furniture stacked high. The spaces were stuffed with smaller objects, the kind of junk that Jiri had hoarded.

There was a dusty cord across the entrance, a little below chest-height. He brushed it as he ducked under, and a bell rang somewhere down inside.

A woman came forward from the shadows. She was twice his age, and so thin it was almost scary. She was in a blue overall coat, sleeves rolled back to show arms that were no more than wrist and sinew, and she wore makeup that had apparently been applied while her mind was elsewhere; it seemed to be off-target by a fraction of an inch, and too bright for the ingrained agony beneath.

'Yes?' she said, and she looked at Rorvik with the wariness of a beaten dog being fed by a stranger.

'I'm not really sure,' he said, aware of how weak an opening it was, 'but I was wondering if . . . '

He was interrupted by a slithering sound and a knock of bone on wood. They both looked towards the pile of furniture as a box was pushed out of the way and a child crawled through the gap. He was about seven years old with the face of an aged monkey, shoeless and sooty from the dark jungle gym through which he'd climbed.

The woman was looking at Rorvik again. He said, 'I'm looking for music.'

The child was on his feet now, watching in silence. The woman said, 'Music all comes from Central, doesn't it?'

'I suppose it does.' There was nothing in the child's eyes that Rorvik could read – no hostility, no respect. It unsettled him. 'But the kind of thing I'm looking for never came from Central. Would you know anything about that?'

It was a narrow line he was treading, throwing out bait whilst trying not to incriminate himself. She said, 'I think there's . . . just wait a moment . . . ' She turned, and shuffled around a corner made by five chairs piled high. Rorvik hung back for a moment, then followed her.

There was a mattress that had been turned onto its side, and she was dragging a box out from behind it. Rorvik went forward to help, but she'd already opened the lid flaps and was rummaging around.

She came out with something, straightened, and held it towards him. It was a narc snuff box, not the cassette he'd expected. It quivered slightly in her thin hand, and out of politeness alone he took it. When he lifted the lid it played a tune, a snatch of about twenty seconds.

The woman was staring at him, waiting to read his reaction. He didn't want the box.

'I'll take it,' he said, hoping his smile didn't look as unreal as it felt.

Credit wasn't used anywhere in the fleamarket, so he paid cash. She insisted on wrapping the box in an irregular sheet of recycled paper.

'We had some written music in here, once,' she said. The man had parted with money. It didn't make him a friend, but at least it lifted him out of a number of suspicious categories.

'Written music?'

'On paper. That's what I was told it was, anyway.'

'Have you still got any?'

She shook her head. 'We burned it all,' she said. 'Couple of winters back. Didn't look like much to me, anyway.'

'Where did you get it from?'

'A clearance. Central was emptying out the East city archives, and everything it didn't want got dumped. It's happened four, five times in the last few years. Be nothing left soon. We go down and sort through the heaps. Sometimes it's useful. Sometimes.'

'Would there be any more? Of this written music, I mean?'

'There was only a bit. And it didn't look much, some sort of code. You could always try.'

The grimy child had disappeared back into the labyrinth. As Rorvik moved back towards the alley with the narc box that he didn't want, he said, 'Would Morden be able to help me?'

'Who?' the woman said blankly. But her trembling increased, until her whole body quivered.

'Nothing,' Rorvik said. 'Just an idea.'

East city archives was in one of the boulevard blocks. Most of the windows were boarded – at least on the lower levels, where underbelly might try to climb in – and only one wing of the building was still accessible. The rest were probably full of crawlers, a great, twittering carnivorous sea waiting for dogs to come sniffing through the cellars or birds to fly in through smashed panes.

He climbed three floors, the first two empty. On the

third, he pushed through a flap-door and emerged into a long, low room. It was lit by overhead fluorescents, but most of them were out. There was a dry, sinus-pinching odour that he couldn't identify.

The nearer shelves were stacked with box files, floor-to-ceiling. Beyond that he could see books, more books than he'd ever come across before. Central's Library had what it called books, text-tapes which you could moderate to cycle at your own speed, but these were the real thing, binders and paper and no video needed.

He coughed to get attention, although he couldn't see anybody. There was a movement way down in the room as someone stepped from an alcove.

'What do you want?' It was a reedy, almost effeminate voice, and it belonged to a hunched man in clothes half a size too big for him. He'd lost some of his hair, and what remained was white.

Rorvik said, 'Is this a library?'

'It's an archive,' the man said, walking down towards him. He had a limp, as if he'd once fallen from a ladder when stretching out too far to replace a volume. Slight limp. Short ladder. 'You know what an archive is?'

'Yes,' said Rorvik, who had really no idea.

Now that the man had a better view of Rorvik, he stopped. Rorvik was an obvious citizen, maybe even an Elite; there was something about the way they were bred; as if they all started out different but were growing into the same family. Citizens in the archive on the last three occasions had resulted in slightly less archive.

'Did Central send you?' he said, and Rorvik shook his head.

'I'm here on my own. I'm looking for written music.'

'Written what?'

'Music, you know . . . '

'I know what music is. You're talking about scores. We had a heap of them upstairs, but they got thrown out the last time Central had a rationalisation purge. The crawlers had chewed them up, anyway.'

'What were they like?'
'Like? The crawlers?'
'The scores.'
'I wouldn't know. Some sort of code. Older than this place, anyway. The paper broke up when you touched it. Why should you be interested?'
Rorvik shrugged. It was a question without an answer. He said, 'Can I have a look around? This is still part of Central, isn't it?'
The man obviously wanted to say no, but Rorvik was citizen. 'Do what you like,' the man said, and he turned and limped off down the alcoves.
For a moment, he was at a loss. He'd at least expected to be guided. In Central itself, there wasn't even any kind of display; you sat in a booth and Central read off your borrowing history before making a selection for you. It guaranteed balance. It made things much easier for Central. He went over to the nearest block of shelves; the box-files were dusty and tightly packed together. He tugged one out and opened the flap, and found that the box was filled with razor-thin flimsy oxide discs. Some special kind of reader needed, obviously, and he didn't have one.
The real books started several rows further along. These shelves weren't so densely stacked, no more than two or three volumes on each shelf. If there was such a disease as a book plague, this archive had suffered an epidemic.
He picked one and opened it. It wasn't a printed text, it was a bound copy of a printout – the narrow oxide guide stripe down the outer edges gave away as much. The page was mainly blocks of numbers set out under headings – demographic breakdowns, he spelt out slowly in his mind. Whatever they were. He flicked a couple more pages, but they were no easier to understand.
Others were no better. They were jargon, language to elevate the banal to a level of mystique; hey, guys, we must be doing something important, it sounds so fucking *obscure*. None of them had pictures, but they mostly had

diagrams. Graph lines, overlapping circles, interlocking spheres with colour shading, blocks marching across the pages with their tops cut like steps. The paper felt dry and slippery, ageless and finished to impress.

Some way along, he felt that he was being watched. Not scanned, like in Central, but actual eyeball-and-neck craning watched. When he turned around, the limping man was there.

'I'm closing up,' he said pointedly.

Rorvik started to nod pleasantly, and then realised that he was getting an unsubtle elbow towards the door.

'But I haven't picked anything out yet,' he said, looking back across the nearest shelves.

'Haven't picked anything out?' the man echoed. 'What do you mean?'

'This is a library, isn't it?'

'An archive,' the man said. 'I told you.'

'And it belongs to the city?'

'Yes.' The man was defintely uncomfortable. He started to hitch his body slightly to get the weight off his bad leg, as if the act might get him some sympathy.

'So, I want to borrow something.' Rorvik looked at the shelves again, and took a step nearer. The man took a step along behind.

'*Borrow* something?' he said, almost in a whine.

'No reason why I can't, is there? I'm a citizen, and I've got a Library card. I want to take out a book. A couple of books.'

'Which one?' the man said, horrified.

It didn't really matter. Anything would do, as long as his Library card number got recorded and eventually passed back to Central. He could boost his attendance record without actually attending, and maybe then the computer would stop making enquiries about him.

'Those two,' he said, and pointed.

The limping man looked. There were twelve bound volumes, all identical and much more handsomely presented than anything else on the shelves. Rorvik was pointing somewhere around the middle, somewhere that would nicely spoil the line of the display, which was exactly what he had in mind.

There was bad grace in the way that the underbelly pulled out volumes four and five and carried them off down the room. Rorvik followed to an alcove that had been turned into something of a nest, and handed over his card. The man wasn't sure what to do; he fussed, he shifted things and then shifted them back, and finally found a card form which looked more or less right. He copied the information across, and then placed Rorvik's registration on top of the books. His hand stayed there for a moment.

'A week,' he said. 'You'll bring them back in a week?'

It was suddenly difficult to be cruel, seeing the real apprehension in the man's eyes. 'I'll look after them,' Rorvik said. Damn it, he didn't even have any intention of *reading* them.

Intention was one thing, but then came boredom. Lin Baxter was being very cool after the episode with the illegal cassette, and so Rorvik found himself alone in the evening. He lay on the bed looking at the ironwork shadows thrown across the ceiling, trying not to listen to the passionate rumblings and gasps from *Her Heart on Her Sleeve* on the video in the next room. He'd checked the stocks in the little kitchen, and there was nothing to get excited about. No sense in going out – he'd walked all day, and the sinews and tendons in his legs still quivered slightly as he lay. He couldn't spend anything, not if he was going to keep his promise to visit Jiri Mondrian; he wasn't sure that he had enough for the whole trip, anyway. It left either the books, or banging his head against the wall. Banging his head came second.

The writing was fairly clear, aimed at the non-specialist. After about half an hour Rorvik was sure that he would have to get the two volumes back to the archive, and fast.

*

Morning. He emerged into the boulevard, and immediately knew something was wrong. A high-sided truck from Central's maintenance division was slewed across the road before the occupied wing of the East City archive, manoeuvred to get the open tailgate as close to the entrance as possible. As he watched, two men in green coveralls stepped out of the building; each had an armload of papers. They carried them across to the truck, where hands reached out. There was a thin river of smoke drifting up from somewhere further along.

Rorvik didn't want to be seen with the books that he was carrying, at least not until he had some idea of what all the activity meant. The nearest building was empty, uncared-for steps leading up to a slide-across metal barrier that had been chained and locked and abandoned many years before. He checked to see if he was being watched. Other than the work party, there seemed to be nobody else in the boulevard. He quickly went up the steps, and slid the books through the barrier; there was just enough of a gap for them to pass, and they were well-covered by the weeds that filled the space behind.

When he got nearer to the archive, it became obvious what was happening. Everything from the shelves was being carried out; the oxide discs were being shaken out of their boxes, and the books were being stripped of their bindings. All of the unnecessary dead weight was thrown onto a bonfire, out on the tarmac in the middle of the boulevard – this was the smoke that he'd seen.

Citizens in the archive – bad luck for the limping man, obviously. He wasn't anywhere around, but he was probably cursing Rorvik as the cause of this new phase of Central's 'rationalisation'.

Rorvik made his way back without being noticed – at least, that's what he hoped. At first he thought of leaving the books where he'd placed them in the derelict porch, but then he might as well have thrown them in the river; the crawlers would have them for sure, shredding them and taking away the tatters for bedding. There was a chance that he'd need them again – keeping quiet would be fine as long as he could hope that Central wouldn't miss the loss of two volumes from the series, but if the computer didn't, and if the archive's records linked his name and number to them – well, he'd at least need *something* to offer as a means of fending away disapproval.

Somewhere safe. The apartment wasn't, and he immediately rejected the idea of asking Baxter to keep them for a few days; as soon as Rorvik appeared in the doorway Baxter would probably exit from the opposite window, and he didn't have a fire escape. Jiri's flat would be out of the question, too – as far as he knew, it had already been re-occupied.

There were lockers in the monorail terminal, but they cost money. Not cash money, but credit – and that meant official records. Unfortunately, he couldn't think of anything better.

Later in the day, as Rorvik was rid of the incriminating books and on his way back to his apartment, the service truck pulled away from the East City archive. It carried the archive's entire stock, reduced to essentials of unbound texts and discs. On the top of the heap were a stack of index cards and a handwritten ledger.

The wagon puttered down the boulevard towards the river and at the end turned towards Central Command. Ten minutes later, the driver reversed his vehicle into a gaping cargo bay in a wall of the main Library and then went and stood outside the bay. As soon as he was clear, a seamless metal door dropped slowly and silently across the open port, and he shrugged and went back to the transport centre.

As shutter and floor met, an identical door at the far end of the bay began to lift, spilling a widening crack of light across the unlit chamber. In the brightness beyond two tanklike service robots blinked to see into the darkness and then stamped forward on their sturdy metal legs. One opened the door at the back of the wagon whilst the other looked inside. On seeing the number of books to be carried it gave a buzz of irritation and clanked off to find a powered cart whilst the other clambered into the wagon and began to rummage. Its boxlike shape was an uneasy fit in the cramped interior but its short and powerful legs allowed it to lean at impossible angles, and within moments it had discovered the index cards and the borrowers' ledger. The robot flipped out a couple of extensions and gathered them in, emerging laden from the wagon as the other robot arrived with the cart.

A brief coded exchange took place, and the robot bearing the index and ledger lumbered off to give the index to the computer whilst the other transferred the books from the wagon to the floating platform.

The computer took perhaps twenty seconds to read through the index cards. This slowness was dictated not by its speed of assimilation but by the danger of the cards overheating with friction. Central mulled over the information for half a second and then turned its attention to the ledger. Here it had difficultly, for the wide variations in style and form of the neatest handwriting greatly taxed its ability to recognise and classify.

Two instructions were then issued. The service robot heard the first and trudged off to help its colleague in vaporising the books. At the second, a hitherto idle teleprinter at the Police Elite building gave a guilty start and began to chatter out a message. An orderly at the far end of the telex room heard the distinctive noise of the Central Command link and hurried down to take the message as soon as it was completed. When the buzzer sounded he tore the sheet off with its three copies and read the top copy through.

'Memo from Central Command,' he read, 'for the attention of Detective Inspector Randall, Central Police Division. Observe and report on the activities of one citizen Lee Rorvik, personal data and history to follow. Recent movements of the subject have given cause for concern with regard to a possibility of civil disobedience.

Act accordingly in the interests of prevention.'

The orderly shrugged. Routine stuff, if a little strong. He split the copies and routed them to the relevant departments.

3

There was, of course, insufficient credit left on Rorvik's card to afford the monorail to the nursing home. The cost of the music box and the charges for the locker had reduced his resources drastically, but a promise was a promise, and he had to find some way to deliver Jiri's bottle. After a calculation which strained his unsteady mathematical abilities he walked three miles to a branch station and joined the monorail there. The cost would empty his account completely, but there was nothing he needed until the payment of the next citizens' bonus.

The convalescents' centre lay amidst the ruins of the old spaceport. The single track of the elevated monorail ran straight towards it, and as the dark towers of the city were left behind it was possible to see the spaceport's old homing beacon beyond the farms and fields like a thread on the horizon.

There was nothing to do but sit on the hard seat and watch the sparse squares of vegetation flickering past. Occasionally there was a wild rocking in the carriage's progress which indicated broken or disjointed plates in the linear accelerator rail, but otherwise the only hook for one's attention was the ever-present piped music which dripped languidly from grilles set into the carriage bulkheads. Rorvik was coming actively to hate such music; in his own mind he compared it to food chewed by somebody else. He looked back down the train. The few passengers were all citizens like himself, but they were sitting quite composed, appearing to think of nothing in particular.

The track swept in a curve around what had once been a blast wall and gradually dropped to ground level. Buildings like the monuments of some ancient necropolis passed close on either side, vanishing abruptly as the carriage hissed into a tunnel and began a silent deceleration.

Rorvik was the only passenger to disembark in the underground station. Although originally designed to handle masses of travellers it was now unattended, and he was left alone as his transport sped away leaving a faint breeze of displaced air to wash along the tunnel. He had made this visit only once before, and had been hopelessly lost for over an hour. This time he was no more certain of his route, but resolved to follow the crudely-painted arrows on the floor. They were colour-coded to indicate the various convalescent homes; he was to follow blue, which led to a depressing and badly-converted engineering shop.

He could identify his target from afar by the music which seeped to him along the tunnel. When he arrived, an unenthusiastic nurse in standard green uniform told him that the patients were all above ground level, taking the air in a blast pit.

The pit was a concave dish perhaps half a mile across. The entrance from below ground was off-centre and heavily shielded, and Rorvik had to walk around this shielding before he was able to see anything or anybody.

The area was dotted with hunched, muffled figures in wheelchairs. They were spread hundreds of yards apart, either unable or unwilling to communicate. The only movement on the horizon was a single green-clad form which moved on a slow patrol some distance away.

As he climbed the shallow slope - now that he thought about it, an ideal trap for any chairbound deserters - the nurse turned and followed his progress with a cold stare.

'You are wasting your time,' she called as soon as he was within earshot. 'This is not a visiting day.'

It had never occured to Rorvik that there might be set days for visitors. 'Please,' he said, 'I've come all the way from the city. I'm looking for a friend, Jiri Mondrian.'

It hardly seemed possible, but her frosty countenance chilled further. 'That is neither here nor there. I've no authority to over-ride standing orders.'

'I used all my credit to get here. It'll be weeks before I can afford to come back.'

She smiled sweetly, and pronounced her next word carefully. 'Tough.' And then she began to walk away. After a few steps she paused, turned and indicated one of the most distant figures in the dish. 'Over there,' she said without warmth. 'You can have five minutes. Then I remove you.' She turned her back, and moved on.

It was a long haul up the slope. Persephone must have been quite something, once, when the spaceport was washed dry by the blasts of landers and the boulevards were crammed with traffic. Now it was an empty nowhere with a weakening sun, not even worth the expense of an offworld defence ring. Anybody wanting to attack would have a Sunday walk, but they'd better not be expecting much when they arrived.

Jiri didn't even hear him coming. He put a hand on the chair - it was a converted trolley from the maintenance workshops - and swung around with a smile ready-pasted and hung up to dry.

He'd got worse, that was obvious straight away. He'd looked like he was ill, but now he looked like he was dying, skinned-down and tight as if in rehearsal. Only Jiri's eyes seemed really alive, clear with a desperation that came from an awareness of the walls which were falling around them.

'Hello, Lee,' he said. 'I didn't think you'd be coming.'

'I made a promise,' Rorvik said, and then realised how bad it sounded; no friendship and no concern, just plain old duty. He went on quickly, 'I brought the bottle.'

'Great. Shall we split?'

'You go ahead.' Rorvik reached inside his jacket, glancing around for the nurse. She wasn't near enough to see.

'No, join me. It'll be the only social life I get.' Jiri took the bottle and raised it; he took no more than a small sip before he broke up coughing. 'God's balls,' he said, 'I'm cured.'

Rorvik pushed away the temptation to give the neck of the bottle a careful wipe. 'How are you feeling?' he said, not sure that he wanted to hear the answer.

'Pretty insecure. They're trying to kill me.'

'The food's so bad, is it?'

'So bad? It's poisoned. I've been watching. Most of the types out here are ancient and on the edge. None of them last more than a couple of weeks; they arrive on stretchers and they leave on trolleys. There are two kitchens, and they're both guarded. For one of them, the staff have to show a pass to get in. When it comes to plates and stuff, they have their own and it's kept separate from anything the patients use. Supplies are delivered in locked vans twice a week.'

'Do you want me to do anything about it?' Rorvik asked uncertainly. He was obviously less than happy about the idea of putting forward such a harebrained complaint.

Jiri looked up at the overcast sky, where Persephone's blood was drying on the clouds. 'Forget it,' he said.

There was a few moments' awkward silence. Rorvik broke it by saying, 'I got your case, like you asked.'

'Thanks. Did you take it home?' Rorvik nodded. 'I suppose that means they've given my place to someone else?'

'As far as I know.'

'Bastards.'

'When I was digging through for the bottle, I found an old cassette. Would you know anything about it?'

'A cassette?'

'An old one. Non-standard.'

'I know it. I found it in the flat when I moved in.'

'Did you ever try to play it?'

'Once. I couldn't get it to fit the machine. Did you?'

'I messed around with it a bit. There was some music on it. Lin's got it, now.' And the river got it shortly after. Rorvik chose a spot on the pockmarked concrete and sat down.

There was another long pause, as they both sat and stared at nothing. Surely there must be more to it, more to say when time was so short; Rorvik found that he was looking out for the nurse, anticipating the moment when she would appear and tell him to go.

Jiri said, 'What else have you been doing?' He could only ask, because he had nothing to offer. Everything that he'd done in the past few weeks was indistinguishable from what he was doing now.

'Got myself turned into a criminal.'

Jiri actually sat up a little. 'A what?'

'I borrowed some stuff from an archive. The idea was that I'd boost my Library attendance record without actually having to go anywhere near Central. I didn't even bother to look at what it was I'd picked, not until I got home, and then I knew I was in trouble.'

'What was it?'

'Two volumes from the report of the social engineers to a sub-committee of the board of Futures, Incorporated.' Jiri looked blank, so he went on, 'The social engineers were the people who cooked up a scheme for the administration of Persephone when Futures pulled out. They were mainly concerned with doing the minimum possible, so that they could save money and still satisfy international law. Establishing Central was the main part of the scheme, and once they'd fixed that they started looking for the cheapest way to set it going.'

'How does this make you a criminal?'

'Maybe it doesn't, I don't know. When I got back, the archive was being emptied out and everything was being taken back to Central. When the machine scans the other ten books, it will spot the gap. And then, if it looks at the records . . .'

'So you borrowed a couple of books. There's nothing wrong in that.'

'Central makes the laws, and that's the problem. Because one of the books was a set of . . . of extrapolations.' The unfamiliar word didn't come out easily. 'International law set a limitation of responsibility on Futures. They had to guarantee stability on Persephone for a minimum period, but as soon as that period expired they didn't have to worry. The extrapolations were to find the cheapest way of doing as little as possible to keep things ticking over for the minimum period.'

'When does it expire?'

'As far as I can tell, it's gone.'

'And everything stays normal.'

'How could we tell? We've never known anything else. But I think I've seen the scheme that Futures decided on.'

'Which is?'

'Set up Central, and make citizens out of all Futures employees. Everybody else becomes . . . well, I suppose they become underbelly. Because social programming comes expensive, don't programme; just set down a few guidelines and let the Central computer programme itself, given the notion of absolute power.'

'It seems to have worked, more or less.'

'You haven't seen the end of the extrapolation. I have. Central's ultimate aim is to use all of its administrative power and media influence to breed the citizens down into a standard social unit.'

'A what?'

'A human statistic. People can't be handled easily in a programme, they don't behave right. Central can't change, because it can't see outside itself. So it's working to change us, instead.'

Randall turned the corner and panted up the last flight of

steps which took him onto the sixth floor of the Police Elite building. In the corridor he placed his sealed briefcase on the floor and took his own pulse; it was pounding hard, he noted with satisfaction. He imagined the hot blood flushing away all the junk in his system.

On the way to his office he passed the row of vacuum elevators. The indicator light over one of the sliding doors lit up, and two officers and a cadet emerged. They had been waiting in the main hall and had seen Randall begin his purposeful trot up the stairs, and now the officers looked curiously after their eccentric fellow whilst the cadet followed the rules of protocol and showed no interest.

Randall kicked his door open and slid gratefully into the corner office. Across the room a younger man quickly removed his feet from the desk and stuffed a bundle of telex forms under his chair, but on recognising Randall he retrieved the documents and placed his footwear back on open view.

'That was fast,' Randall said, and his junior nodded without smiling. 'Who were you expecting?'

'I've been practising,' Killoran replied. 'It might have been somebody important.'

'Well, thanks.' Randall contemplated his mess of a desk for a moment and then swept all the papers to one end in order to make a clear space. He set the briefcase down and then rummaged in an equally untidy drawer for the key. When the seal was finally broken he extracted two cans – the case's only contents – and tossed one across to Killoran.

Killoran read, 'Squeeze. The Citizen's Beer,' and looked up in surprise. 'Where did you get this?' he asked.

'Ask no questions,' Randall replied. 'There are ways and means.'

They peeled the tops off the cans and drank. Killoran grimaced. 'Now I remember why I left all this behind.'

'Rough stuff, isn't it?' Randall choked, and thought of all the goo inexorably re-clogging his system. 'How could you face going into a bar and saying to the 'tender, "Gimme a squeeze"?'

Killoran nodded, again without any trace of a smile. He smiled as often as the snows fell in summer.

They threw the empty cans down the incinerator chute and heard them rattle down the full length of the building. 'Should clear any old blockages,' Randall observed. Then he turned back into the office. 'Anything new?'

'How would I know?'

'Because you come in early every morning and read the telexes before I arrive.'

With no obvious reaction of guilt, Killoran said 'There's a direct memo from Central Command. It's been lying in the traffic control "in" tray for the last twenty-four hours.'

'What reason?'

'It was directed to you by name only. No department. The orderly thought you were in traffic control still and routed it there.'

'Why didn't they use an up-to-date directory?'

'They're always being pinched. No honesty in this place.'

Randall searched out the memo from an intidy pile and ran his eyes over it. 'Have you read this?' he said without looking up.

'In the lift.'

'Naughty.' Randall turned the name over in his mind. 'Lee Rorvik. Do we know him?'

'I shouldn't think so. Central would have given us the security computer reference.'

'I was just testing you.' No he wasn't, he'd forgotten. '"Observe and Report", it says. Have we got the personal data?'

Killoran crossed and sorted through yet another pile of papers. 'Somewhere in here. There's also a mention in the daily bulletin. A connection with some missing printed material from one of the old archives. It seems to have been loaned on Rorvik's Library card number.'

'Probably connected. I suppose we'll have to go and see him. Can't see the need for such a strong directive though.'

There was a single knock on the door, and it opened a few inches. An orderly's head poked through the crack. 'Just arrived for you, sir.' Two feet below the head a hand appeared with another telex copy.

'This, you may note, is not traffic control,' Randall said.

All that was visible of the head blushed, and Killoran reached over for the paper. 'That wasn't me, sir.' But the denial lacked conviction.

Killoran read it and held it out for Randall, who waved it away. 'Just tell me what it says.'

'It's from Central again. Security section. It's instructing that Rorvik should be a Grade Two operation.'

Randall was upright and reaching for his phone, all expectations of a quiet afternoon gone. A Grade Two was big, and already there was a twenty-four hour delay. As he punched out the Services number, he told Killoran, 'Get onto Stores and fix us up with some radios.'

'Any weapons?'

'Not for a Grade Two. Just the radios.' Then Services came on the line, and he began to list his requirements. There was some argument which was solved by the mention of the Grade Two. Halfway through, he broke off and said to Killoran 'When you're done there, run a check on Rorvik's recent credit uses. See if there's anything recorded for today, and find out where.'

Killoran went off to the input room and Randall continued with his list, his eyes focussed far outside the window. A Police Elite helicopter was beating its way steadily across the rooftops towards the headquarters. Almost as an afterthought, Randall added, 'See if you can fix me up with a 'copter as well. One with a searchlight. And I want a fairly responsible pilot, if that's not a contradiction. Not like the idiot who got himself killed on the bravado run last week.'

As he put the phone down Killoran returned from the input room. 'He's been using the monorail today. Out to the old spaceport where the nursing homes are.'

'Good. Get a couple of men on the station, see if they can

spot him when he comes back. I'll go and have a quick shave before we go over to his apartment. It may be a long night.'

As two cadets hurried to the city's main terminus, Rorvik was walking back from the branch station on the city's outskirts. He was uncomfortably close to the underbelly here, and he was glad to leave its fringes behind and approach comparative civilisation.

The city was in the long shadows of late afternoon when he arrived within sight of Central Command. He didn't particularly want to go home, but he couldn't think of anything else to do at this time so he stayed by the river and called into a citizens' cantina to eat. Although it wasn't a busy time his Library card was waved away as he offered it for registration, so he slipped it back into his pocket and carried his tray through into the main hall.

A handful of citizens was scattered about the hall, some in small groups but mostly alone. The inevitable music was leaking in from all corners, and over by a window looking out onto the water Rorvik recognised Baxter, the remains of his meal on the table before him and next to that a stack of Library cassettes. Rorvik went over and sat down opposite.

'Dreaming?' Baxter gave a start and turned.

'What? Oh . . . hello. I'm sorry, I didn't see you,' he said, but his manner was unconvincing.

'You're not still nervous about us playing that cassette, are you?'

Baxter looked around hurriedly to see if anybody had heard. There was no-one within earshot, but a short Drone robot was stumping down towards them, clearing tables on its way. 'What do you mean, *us*?' he hissed, as if the robot might listen. '*I* was the one who took it and dumped it in the river.'

'All right, then. You're not still nervous about *me* running the cassette.'

Baxter shook his head, afraid to speak as the Drone came

level with their table and reached for his empty plate. It cleared before him and then, with a practised tweak, it snapped Rorvik's full plate from under his nose and emptied it into its hopper.

Rorvik threw his cutting fork down and it collected that, too, and then waddled off cheerfully. He watched it go in blank resignation – the afternoon with Jiri had worn the edge off his appetite. Baxter was looking out of the window again; it was possible to see down the river as far as Central's dome.

There might be trouble ahead, Rorvik thought, and it gave him a queasy twisting feeling inside. The records would go back to Central, and then Central would cross-check them, and then ... what? Maybe nothing. He'd never heard of a rule specifically proscribing information on Central's origins, but that was probably because Central had ensured that nothing was available. And as for disciplining of a citizen ... he'd never heard of that, either. Underbelly who offended were simply made to disappear ... when they could be caught by the Elite, that is, and most weren't. Exactly where those who disappeared went to, nobody knew; there were rumours of detention camps way out in the ice belt, but if they existed it was a one-way trip with no appeals.

Citizens didn't need to be disciplined, because citizens didn't offend. They were monitored and controlled, guided and chided, led by the nose from the baby farm to the bonfire. Long after three weeks of work by Futures' social engineers, the dawn of the grey harvest was only hours away.

Maybe Central could strip away his privileges and toss him over to the underbelly, but it could never erase his breeding or the knowledge which made him ... what, dangerous? He'd never thought of himself as dangerous before. It sat wrong, like someone else's old clothes. If Central was going to judge him, it would be the ice belt. Or maybe even the bottom of the river. In all the dying city there was nowhere he could hide, nowhere he wouldn't be spotted and reported. The underbelly might hold him for a while, but only as long as the money lasted.

'What's under there, do you think?' he said suddenly, and Baxter looked around at him.

'Under where?'

'Central.'

Another glance down the river, and then Baxter was looking at Rorvik again. 'Cellars or something, I suppose,' he said. 'How would I know?'

'It can't be cellars. The river goes underneath.'

'There's your answer, then.' Baxter turned in his seat as Rorvik stood and stepped out into the aisle. 'Where are you going?' he said.

'Just for a walk,' Rorvik called as he moved away. 'See you around.'

He climbed the protective wall and dropped the few feet on the other side to the embankment. The curve of the dome stretched up and away from him, but from here he could see the poured-stone base of the structure that was normally hidden. The river was broad, and disappeared into a slot which ran most of the width of the building. An overgrown path led to the very edge of the water, and through the weeds broken concrete showed like patches of bone.

The boom and splash of the flow overpowered all other sounds as Rorvik crouched on the bank and looked into the darkness. A weir of metal railings was trapping driftwood and debris across the low tunnel mouth. He couldn't see more than two or three feet inside, but he could feel the low rumbling echo which told him that there was space and distance in the darkness.

It didn't look very inviting. He was ready to abandon the whole idea with relief, but some of the rails out across the weir had corroded almost through. In one place a beam of driftwood had lodged, and its rocking motion as the water buffeted it had levered one rail out of line. He could walk out along the horizontal as easy as anything, the surface of the river a couple of feet below him, and holding the rails would keep him balanced. Now that he'd come so far, there was no excuse for him not to swing out and across and then put his head inside for a look.

Even as he transferred his weight out onto the weir, he knew that he wasn't going to see anything useful – if he saw anything at all. He'd been hoping to see some shelter, somewhere clean and crawler-free that he could move the books to and keep in his mind as a secret bolt-hole for if things got rough; a part of his mind was insisting that they wouldn't, the blinkered-optimist part of the imagination that everybody turns to when they can't handle what's going to happen.

The metal of the weir started to groan, and on the next step he felt it give. The structure was too weakened to take him; it was fine near the bank, but towards the middle it was too much. That was all he needed; for a moment he peered through the bars, but there was still nothing to see. He was reaching out to start moving back when the tie-rail broke away from under him.

He hadn't been bothering to keep much of a hold with his free hand, and when he felt himself falling and made a desperate grab he closed on empty air. The tie-rail hadn't snapped clean but had just bent enough to drop him; it was the last thing he saw before the cold water shocked him into stupidity.

The chimes rang at the door, and Louann Roget ignored them. When they rang again she turned up the volume of the video to cover the sound.

Out in the corridor, Randall heard the boost in sound and turned to Killoran. 'You hear that?' he said. 'She's home, all right.'

Killoran nodded agreement, not wishing to speak in case he should sound breathless from the climb up the stairs.

'Give it a knock,' Randall said. 'She'll hear that.' Killoran knocked, at first politely and then an angry hammer as the volume inside the apartment was raised again. Randall smiled. 'Keep it up,' he said.

After a few seconds, the passionate strains of 'Her Heart on Her Sleeve' were cut short, allowing the easy melody of the corridor background music to filter through. Killoran stopped his hammering and the door swung open.

Louann saw two men, one slightly older, both citizens. But no; there was something different. Their dress was nonstandard, and of an expensive-looking cut. Police Elite. As if in confirmation, the older one smiled and said, 'Good evening, Ms Roget. We're security officers. Show her your card, Killoran.' The younger one stepped forward and to one side of her, holding out an official-looking security pass.

Randall stepped forward on the other side, so that Louann turned when he spoke. 'We'd like to speak to Rorvik, if you don't mind.' Killoran slipped behind her and into the room.

'But ... he isn't here.'

'That's all right, Ms Roget. We don't mind waiting. May we come in?'

'Well, I'm not sure I ... '

Killoran spoke from within the apartment. 'Very nice home you have here, Ms Roget,' he said, looking at the bare walls and the standard video.

Louann spun round in surprise, and Randall stepped into the room and closed the door behind him. She struggled for a moment to grasp the situation, and then accept it. 'Well,' she said, 'won't you sit down?'

'Why, thank you,' said Randall, and led her over to the plain divan which was the room's only furniture beside the video surround. As she settled uncertainly he glanced up at Killoran. 'Neil, have you thought that Ms Roget might like some coffee?'

'I'm sorry,' she said. 'I supposed I ought to have offered.'

Killoran gave her a reassuring smile and moved towards what he knew from the standard design must be the kitchen. 'Just leave it to me,' he said.

'There's only ersatz,' she called after he had gone through the door. 'It's all I can get.'

Killoran shouted something muffled and incomprehensible, and Randall leaned forward to speak in low, confiding tones. 'Now, Ms Roget, I expect you're wondering what all this is about.'

'I'm rather confused. I was in the middle of . . . ' A loud smash of dropped crockery came from the kitchen. The door opened a crack.

'Nothing broken,' Killoran said cheerfully, and the door closed again.

'To begin with,' Randall went on, 'I don't want you to worry. Lee Rorvik isn't hurt, and he hasn't done anything wrong.'

She was confused. 'Then what's the matter?'

'Well, it concerns some information from one of the old archives. We're in the process of transferring the last ones to microfilm in Central command, and I suppose you can guess what it must be like. Some of the stuff hasn't been looked at in years. Anyway, when we came to check through the catalogues it seems there was some material that should never have been available, and furthermore it seems that Lee Rorvik has come by this information somehow.'

She was trying to take an interest, he could tell, but it was as if she were dragging her mind back from a place far away. 'And what is this material, Mr . . . '

'It's Randall. I'm an Inspector. I can't actually answer that as it's got a security classification, but I'm sure we can clear it up very quickly. When are you expecting him back?'

She shrugged. 'I wouldn't know.'

A prompt, maybe. He said, 'We know he used the mono. Now we know that he's back in the city.'

She met his eyes without guilt or concern. 'So what?' she said.

The surface was like mercury. It bounced and sparkled just

out of reach, and as the sparkling died he knew that he was being pulled under Central. Then a quick eddy flipped him over, and he lost it altogether for a formless green that had no apparent depth or texture; something rushed out of it and banged him hard, and as the current dragged him over the obstruction he lost most of the breath that he'd managed to hold.

His hand broke out into the air for a moment, he was sure, but when he struggled to find the surface all he could manage was a slow, ineffective threshing, all of his strength compressed and made useless. He could be ploughing his way deeper. He needed to open his mouth and gulp, air or water, it didn't seem to matter any more – anything just to wash away the pain in his lungs.

No, he tried to tell his body, wait for air. Forget it, his body said, I gotta *breathe*.

There was stone against his head, and it was hard; he bounced and skittered along it, shoulder, elbows, knuckles, and then was suddenly whirled around and let go.

He was in near-still water, and rising. He broke surface through a loose crust of debris.

Something out there was firm, because it didn't bob and sink when he grabbed it; there wasn't much purchase for his fingers, but he was desperate enough to grip glass. He dragged himself over, and his head clear of the water.

He spat out a mouthful of slime. Two or three minutes of panting and retching passed before his interests began to widen.

The lights which had at first been swimming at the backs of his eyes now resolved themselves into dancing patterns of reflected water, light from upriver some distance away. He'd been siphoned off into a little sargasso basin of still water, a heaving skin of green scum clogged with anything that would float; box lids, driftwood, cans, and Lee Rorvik.

It was a small harbour, a cutout into the embankment wall. The walls on three sides rose sheer and higher than he could see, but there were steps cut into the back wall which led down to a marina jetty, berths for maybe four boats with walkways around and between them. The jetty was mostly rotted-through and collapsed; Rorvik was between an unattached cross-beam and the tilted hull of a sunken vessel. When he felt strong enough, he started to pull himself along to where the jetty still looked firm; the surface debris plucked and clawed at him as he moved.

He stood on the marina walkway, dripping and shivering. The wood was cankerous with wet rot, and when he started forward he tested every step before he put his weight down. Once he was on stone he felt safer; it was green and slick, but at least it wasn't likely to open up underneath him.

Climbing the steps, he left some of the noise of the river behind. From here it seemed sluggish, almost placid, a slow black muscle easing its way along down below. Rorvik squinted to make the most of the light.

The embankment was a broad promenade with the level of the river about twenty yards below and screened by an ornate parapet. Knowing the size of Central it must have stretched ahead for quite a distance, but the shimmering twilight failed to illuminate its full length. At intervals marching off into the darkness were decorated metal streetlamps, encrusted with the same thick moss which coated the stonework. Far away, like a bright star on a summer night, a single light-source burned against the low concrete roof.

Rorvik found it difficult to keep his footing on the slime. When he tried to stand still he had no grip, yet when he walked it was like a thick jam dragging at his feet. It grew sparser as he moved downstream and it was starved of even the meagre glow of reflected sunlight. Plaques and signs on walls which had previously been too overgrown to read were now obscured by the dark.

The light-source proved to be an open trap in the roof. Rorvik dropped behind the parapet as he saw activity beyond it, stocky service robots of a type he had never seen coupling links onto a broad tube. They lifted it and tottered to the edge under its weight, pausing for a second and then heaving it out to snake down and then impact on the hard surface of the river. Something tugged at the leg of Rorvik's slacks and he brushed it away unconsciously.

A throbbing began in the red haze beyond the trap, and a cluster of searchlights flared into life, their beams converging on the point where tube and water met. The effect was of a sudden brilliance flooding the whole riverside, and from the shadows loomed the great rusting hulk of an old ship. It was turned on its side with its decks half underwater, a mass of bright details and sharp shadows illuminated from above.

The tugging came again at his leg. Again he brushed at it, but this time the action registered in his conscious mind and he looked down in alarm as there was a sharp pain and his hand withdrew, running with blood from a quarter-inch slice.

The animal withdrew out of his reach, tiny red eyes burning with hunger. It retreated no further, but hovered and watched. It was a crawler.

For some reason, he'd never even thought to see a crawler down here; they belonged to buildings and empty housing blocks, moving in a silent tide to occupy space that people had deserted. If there was one, there had to be more.

A movement to his left. Three of them advanced and froze on that side. When he looked back to the first creature, there were five. More were creeping up from behind.

The front ranks made a ring, and the ring filled out. The crawlers made no noise, but a dry scratching of tiny nails on stone ate away at the edge of perception. Rorvik knew that warm bodies were gathering, out there in the darkness.

They watched him; so much meat, and so vulnerable, and the group mind seemed to be weighing the best plan for bringing it down without injury to the pack. Fast and final, and then the blood feast.

Rorvik straightened, slowly. His wet clothes moved against his skin, cold and sticky. The parapet behind gave him no room to back off. As he put a hand back to steady himself on it, one of the crawlers broke ranks and dived for his leg.

Rorvik kicked at the tiny yawn of pink and felt the head snap back and the body jerk behind it. Instantly they were all on him in a wave, yelling like an angry cloud. It was hard to stand under their weight but he did, and fast. They clung to his clothes and dragged him over again. He felt a hard stab as several of the crawlers were mashed against the parapet, and he tried to batter more of them against it.

His arms were up to protect his neck and face, but bites were beginning to tear through his clothing and nip at the skin. Again he threshed against the parapet and half a dozen more fell dead whilst the living crawlers caught the twitching bodies and tores at them indiscriminately. He hurled himself at the stonework and it gave way at last, old mortar powdering and grinding.

This time, he was ready; he had all of the gut-jerking fall with crawlers raining down around him to draw breath and hold it.

Even so, he almost lost it when he hit and went under, but he kept his sense of up and down and was able to strike for the surface immediately. No crawlers came up around him, and already the bank was far behind; on the other side the tilted ship was sliding past as the river carried him high down its centre. He didn't have to swim, all he had to do was keep his head up – difficult enough, but not so hard when he considered drowning as the alternative.

He was beached on a mudflat within sight of the exit weir. He didn't realise at first how close he was; in the time that he'd been under Central the sun had more or less set, and as he waded in the knee-high filth he almost walked into the bars before he saw them. There was no need to force a gap, because he could duck under, after which he only had to stumble through the reeds to get himself to the levee on Central's seaward side.

He got back to the residential section looking like the Mud Monster. The blocks had originally been thrown up fast and cheap as quarters for Futures employees, none of them much more than half a dozen levels high; as a concession to corporate image they'd been given decent frontages with broad steps and a gesture at a porch. He was climbing the steps when he thought of Collinson staring, the elevator out of order, a long climb and maybe having to explain why the Mud Monster was haunting the block stairs. About the books and about his fears of reprimand he gave no thought at all. He decided to go around the building and pull down the counterweighted ladder on the fire escape.

From across the street he was watched by two men in a doorway as he trotted down the front steps and went round to the side of the block. One of them raised a hand radio and pressed the 'transmit' button. 'Unit One to the Great White Chief,' he said, and his companion suppressed a snort.

Up in the fifth-level kitchen Killoran hastily adjusted the volume control on his radio. He paused, but the low hum of conversation from the next room continued uninterrupted. 'Cut the comedy,' he whispered, 'and keep the noise down. Randall's in the next room with the subject's woman.'

'This low enough? Rorvik's left the entrance hall and he's coming up by the fire escape. That means he'll have to get in by a window on your western side.'

Killoran frowned. Which way was west from here? 'What about Unit Two?' he demanded.

In an idling 'copter two blocks away, a nervous cadet responded as the pilot yawned and stretched. 'Unit Two. We're ready to put the lights on him if he goes onto the roof.'

The fire escape was an added complication they could do without. 'Unit One,' Killoran said, 'where is he now?'

'Fourth floor,' the voice came again over the radio. 'That's the one below the fifth.' There was a badly-stifled grunt of malicious glee in the background, but Killoran didn't hear it as he threw the kitchen door open and stepped into the main room.

'Change of plans,' he interrupted sharply. 'Fire escape. Right now.'

Randall turned to Louann. 'Where's the access to the fire escape?'

'It's through his bedroom,' she replied, bewildered. 'Over there. Why . . . '

Rorvik froze, his hand on the door panel and half into the room. He saw the two men swivel and dive towards him and he stepped smartly back and slammed the door in their faces.

Randall grabbed the radio from Killoran and pointed to the door. 'Break it down,' he said, and thumbed the 'transmit' button. 'This is Randall to all units. Rorvik's on the fire escape and running.'

Louann half-rose from the divan in horror as the bedroom door bulged and splintered under Killoran's repeated kicking. On the next kick it burst and sprang inward to an empty room and a half-open window.

'Unit One,' Randall called. 'Where are you now?'

'We're at the bottom of the fire escape,' came the reply, suddenly competent. 'He'll have to pass us if he comes down.'

'One of you stay there, the other one cover the main entrance. Let's have the 'copter over the roof and get some lights on the place. Unit One, start climbing now. We'll force him up to the roof and trap him.'

Like a great mantis the 'copter reared from behind the building opposite, all lights blazing. The glare slid across the bedroom window and off into the night.

'You're going to the wrong bloody building!' Randall roared. 'Get back over here!'

The 'copter made a nose-around correction. The cadet was trying to apologise, and in the background the pilot was shouting 'They all look the same from up here!'

'This is no damn use at all!' the voice of the man on the fire escape cut across the frequency. 'You're casting too many shadows. I can't see a thing.'

The pilot in the background began to get aggressive, but Randall stopped them all with a loud burst of feedback by pressing the *transmit* button without disengaging the receiver. As their ears rang from the piercing tone he said 'Now hear this. I want the 'copter to hover at roof level and wait for Rorvik to emerge. Unit One is to continue ascent until you've swept him up there. Is that plain?'

Unit One sounded doubtful. 'What if he gets in on another level?'

'That's *my* problem. I've got all exits covered and enough men to search the building. If necessary I'll do it.' For the first time he noticed Louann's inert form on the floor by the divan. He looked up at Killoran. 'Have you bopped her one?'

Killoran gave a reasonable impression of being affronted. 'Certainly not. She fainted.'

'That's all we need. Put her somewhere out of the way, then.' She groaned as Killoran lifted her, sacklike, and dumped her on the divan. 'Better give her a glass of water as well, or whatever it is you're supposed to do.'

'Right.' As Killoran disappeared into the kitchen Louann opened her eyes and tried to focus.

'What's happening to me?' she gasped.

'To you, nothing,' Randall snapped, the fatherly manner completely evaporated. 'Keep your head down and you'll be all right.'

Killoran returned with the water as the radio came back to life. 'This is Unit One. I've reached the roof and there's no sign of Rorvik.'

'Could you have missed him?'

'I doubt it, but anything's possible with this fly-boy buzzing around overhead blinding me.'

'Keep your complaints for afterwards. Get back down the fire escape and check all the adjacent windows. I'll get a search carried out on the inside.' Randall gave a series of rapid instructions to several units waiting out of sight at ground level. Out of the corner of one eye he saw across the bedroom his man on the fire escape go past the window and down without pausing; and then he gave a second, more careful look to make sure it wasn't Rorvik. It wasn't. He looked back from the shattered doorway as Killoran let in one of his men from the outside corridor.

'We've done the search, sir,' the man said. 'Cleared every room on this side of the building apart from the one directly below this. Tenant name of Gerrard. The caretaker says that Rorvik knows him.'

Louann had vanished into the bathroom and was being loudly sick. Randall said, 'This could be it. Come on, Neil.' And they followed the messenger down to the fourth floor.

Rorvik released a pent-up breath and stepped from behind the bedroom door. There were voices off down the corridor and retching sounds from the bathroom, but otherwise he was alone.

He was sure he could forget any ideas of escape through the building, thick as it was with the Police Elite. On the roof he knew there were several planks and ladders, part of an old and forgotten scaffolding. One or more of them might be long enough to bridge to the next roof; on one side the building was very close indeed, only a narrow alley away, and as long as the plank didn't snap with his weight in the middle . . .

He cautiously poked his head out of the window and looked around. The fire escape was deserted now, and the 'copter was scanning the surrounding streets with its underslung searchlights. He hopped quickly over the sill and disappeared into the night.

Collinson was waiting outside Gerrard's door when Randall and Killoran arrived, his passkey held proudly aloft. In spite of the urgency Randall insisted on the formalities, showing Collinson his security clearance and then waiting as he read it with painful slowness.

As the fields disengaged they kicked the door open and plunged into the room together, closely followed by the other officer and then, at a more cautious pace, the caretaker. Killoran went straight across to the window whilst Randall and the other man checked the adjacent rooms. A new-looking Public Broadcast receiver was belting out loud music in the corner, and Killoran switched it off before he spoke.

'Rorvik didn't come in here,' he said. 'The window catches have been painted over. God help Gerrard if there's a fire.'

Randall looked around. 'Where is Gerrard, anyway? The other rooms are empty.'

'Over here, sir,' the other officer called from beside the divan. 'He slipped underneath. He's ... '

'Dead drunk.' Killoran held up an empty can of "Squeeze; the Citizen's Beer" and then let it fall onto a heap of others just like it. 'No wonder he slept through the search.'

'Damn,' said Randall, 'I think he's slipping away from us.' A sudden thought occurred. 'I can't hear the 'copter.'

Killoran looked out of the window. 'He's moved off the roof.'

Randall took the quietly hissing radio off its clip inside his tunic and switched to *transmit*. 'Unit two,' he called, 'what are you playing at?'

The cadet's voice came faintly. 'We're checking the streets around the block. I thought ... '

'Don't think. Get back over the roof.'

Killoran said, 'What now?'

'We'll just have to seal the building and take it apart. We know he's still in it, somewhere.'

'Do we, though?'

Randall shook his head angrily. 'We have to start with something. The place is ringed, so what else have we got? We'll start by going over Rorvik's place.' Killoran followed him up the stairs, leaving Collinson and the officer to carry Gerrard through to his bed.

Two floors above them Rorvik dragged the tarpaulins off old timber. He was alone on the roof, but could hear desperate activity in the street below as newly-arrived wagons poured men into the building.

There were two ladders, and neither of them looked particularly strong. They were, however, a better proposition than the planks, which were rotten and splintering. He hauled out the sturdier of the two and carried it over to the edge, laying it down carefully before taking a cautious look down.

Damn! There were two officers in the narrow alleyway seven floors below. One of them was playing a torch over the blank side of the building, its beam narrow and bright like a laser. Rorvik would easily be spotted as he crossed the gulf against the night sky. Damn and double-damn.

A raving clatter as the 'copter popped into view from behind the block across the street, and then it was floating and weaving across to him. Cover on the roof was virtually nil; he would be seen as soon as lights were brought to bear and then he would be gathered in as easily as a crawler in an empty swimming pool.

The cadet fiddled awkwardly with the beam direction controls, so that the lights swung across the roof and then shot off the edge.

'Get those beams back on there!' the pilot shouted into his headset. 'I think I saw him!'

The cadet tried to respond but over-corrected and shot off the other side, so the pilot raised the nose of the craft and angled in closer to tighten the field of view. A bitter wind fanned the surface of the roof as they dropped towards it, and the cadet turned and fumbled for a hand-torch. 'I'll tell Randall,' he shouted as the little unit powered up.

The pilot shook his head emphatically. 'Be sure first.'

The hand beam flickered where the big lights were too cumbersome to point, dancing over angles and shadows. 'I think I see something,' the cadet called. 'Front of the building, near the edge.'

The pilot nodded and made the minute adjustments necessary to start a slow drift across to where the cadet was pointing. The shadows foreshortened and changed their shape as the light moved over them, and then the 'copter's plastic bubble abruptly crazed in a localised starburst.

'He threw something!' the cadet yelled. The pilot made no response but trod hard on his rudder-bar to whip the tail around and get away from the roof. He had no wish to go straight up and expose the fragile underside of his machine to further attack.

As the tail scythed towards him, Rorvik threw the ladder again. It travelled straight upward and the tail smacked into it below the middle and flipped it over, the lower end arcing up and into the blinding whirl of the rotors. Matchwood was instantly everywhere, accompanied by a scream of protesting metal as the rotors shattered and the 'copter's engine accelerated to an impossible speed without their drag. The whole vehicle flopped heavily onto the edge of the roof and balanced momentarily before the counterbalancing torque of the tailblade swung it around with agonising slowness until the greater part of its weight hung in space over the street.

It tumbled, as inevitably it must, taking a sizeable bite of masonry with it. The pilot fought with the controls all the way down, but without the rotors they were quite dead. He knew it, but simply didn't want to believe it. Windows flipped past and upward as if seen from an elevator, and the cadet covered his eyes and face with folded arms as they'd shown him in survival school.

They landed on the roof of a Police Elite wagon, crushing it instantly. Both vehicles ignited and burned with an explosion that broke every window on the front of the block and several in the block opposite. There were a couple of minor explosions, and then the wreckage settled to a regular and even conflagration.

Voices raised in panic, anger, despair – they all drifted up to Rorvik, crouching numbed by the chewed-open gap in the parapet. Raising himself slightly and looking down he could see distant figures below weaving in a frantic ring around the disaster.

He arose stiffly and crossed to the alleyway side. Down below the two officers were running, as probably everybody else in the building was, towards the scene of the fire.

The other ladder was of doubtful safety, but under the circumstances that was irrelevant. Fully extended its tip barely rested on the low wall across the gap, but a short plank wedged between the bottom rung and the near edge gave some guarantee against slipping.

Rorvik was unworried, only mechanically attentive, his entire stock of fear and apprehension emptied and dried out. He barely saw the abyss beneath as he straddled the ladder and pulled himself along, hardly heard the creaks of danger as his weight came fully onto the braced joint in the middle.

Down below, the street was as bright as day. Despite the immense heat Randall felt a chill of anger as he descended the open steps and looked onto the wreckage. Killoran breathlessly caught up a few seconds later.

'Accident, chief? Or Rorvik?'

'I don't know.' Randall suddenly frowned at the size of the crowd jabbering before the fire. 'Who's watching the back of the building? And what about the fire escape?'

Several officers shuffled and looked away, but one stepped forward. 'I was on the back, sir,' he said. 'We all heard the bang and came to see if we could help.'

'Well, you can't. Get back to your posts.'

A large number of the men began to disperse reluctantly. Randall felt weary, and not from running down the stairs. 'Two 'copters in one week,' he said, mostly to himself. 'There goes next year's budget.' He turned to Killoran. 'Why, Neil? It was a routine pickup. All you need is a car and a polite manner. Instead we get a Grade Two directive from the computer and . . . and *this*.' His broad gesture included the entire street.

Around and in the alleyway two officers moved back

into position with a hand-beam and resumed scanning the side of the building. There was nothing above them but the night sky and the stars.

4

With the escalation of the operation Randall could easily have requisitioned a helicopter to take him out to the spaceport, but he could raise no enthusiasm for the idea. He disliked them at the best of times; even more, he disliked the young pilots, an élite within an élite. Their psychoprofiles were carefully inspected before training, and they were chosen on the basis of a certain irregularity or imbalance which was fed by the exhilaration of flight to the extent that pilots became almost a part of their machines, unable to think coherently or express themselves except through the controls. Randall said it only confirmed his own opinion, that you had to be mad to fly one of those things.

Instead he took the mono, as Rorvik had done the day before. He also lost his way leaving the station as Rorvik had. After a number of false starts and requests for directions he emerged into the open blast pit and scanned the horizon for the nurse in charge.

There she was, patrolling the huddled mummies on the far side of the bowl. She saw him and stopped, but made no move to approach; instead she stared as he crossed towards her. 'You are wasting your time,' she recited. 'This is not a visiting day.'

'I'm not a visitor,' he replied, and produced his security pass. A slight flick of the eyes and she had read it. 'I understand,' he went on, 'there's a Jiri Mondrian staying here. I'd like to speak to him.'

She smiled her sweet, killing smile. 'I would dearly like to help you, Mr . . . Randall, was it? But I'm afraid it's out of the question.'

'I do have the necessary security clearances from the computer . . . '

'You don't understand,' she cut in. 'Mr Mondrian departed this life at six-thirty this morning.' One or two of the nearer figures stirred, taking an interest. 'Look, we're rather public here. Won't you come down to the office?'

She led him to an office next to what had once been an engineering hangar. A broad window had looked out onto what had been workshops beneath, but these were now badly-lit dormitories and the window was painted over. Randall was shown to an armchair with sagging springs, and the nurse perched behind her desk and began to sort through the envelopes in her 'out' tray.

'This is much better,' she said. 'I know there was nobody nearby, but some of the deaf ones can lip-read, and before you knew it would be all over the grounds. In most cases we can stop it by taking their spectacles away. The file on Mondrian should be in here somewhere . . . '

She removed several sheets of paper from one of the envelopes and began to skim through them.

Randall shifted in the uncomfortable seat. 'You say he died this morning.'

She nodded, still reading. 'At six-thirty. Very inconvenient. Any deaths over the late shift period and we only have a skeleton staff to deal with them.' Randall smiled politely, but she didn't look up; perhaps it hadn't been a joke, after all. 'It's a matter of economics,' she went on. 'Our budget is very limited and we have to plan carefully. Already we're having to cut our convalescence time down to three weeks.'

That didn't sound right. 'You mean . . . after three weeks you send them home?'

'Certainly not. We bury them.'

'*Bury* them?'

Her patience bordered on sarcasm. 'That is the usual procedure with the dead.'

'But what if they're getting better?'

'Then we just have to increase the dosages. There is a demand for our beds, you know.'

Randall was struggling with the concept.

'Wait a minute. Are you telling me that you poison your patients?'

'Certainly not. The kitchens do it for us.'

'The kitchens?'

She laid the papers down on the desk. 'Inspector ... Randall, was it? I can't think you're so naive as to believe that we would force the infirm to suffer. We do it with full authority from Central Command. It's filed in the banks as the voluntary euthanasia programme.'

'So it is voluntary, then?'

'Of course. They eat of their own free will.'

'Knowing it to be poisoned?'

The nurse's eyebrows lifted in surprise. 'Certainly not. What kind of euthanasia programme do you think we'd have then?'

Randall shook his head in disbelief. 'I never knew any of this before,' he said.

'Central Command works in a mysterious way, Inspector Randall, its wonders to perform,' she replied smugly.

Randall thought for a moment. 'Was there a special instruction of any kind regarding this particular patient? Although it's really one of his friends that we're interested in.'

'Now you mention it, there was.' She picked out one of the sheets from the pile. 'There was a direct instruction from Central last night to increase dosage. That's quite unusual.'

'Did you question it?'

'Certainly not. We carried it out.'

That was logical. 'This friend. I believe he was up here yesterday.'

'That's right. Yesterday morning. It was very irregular.'

'Did he bring anything with him?'

Did Randall detect a guilty response as she began shuffling the papers before her? 'No,' she said. 'He brought him nothing.'

'Nothing like a book? You know, paper and bindings? Or a parcel about – ' he spread his hands ' – this size?'

Her discomfort settled, and she was the iron lady again. 'No. Certainly nothing that size.'

Randall was worried. It was almost as if Central Command wanted to interfere with its own instruction. Why remove Rorvik's only visible confidant before he could be interviewed?

'It seems I've had a wasted journey, then,' he said as he levered himself out of the chair. He'd almost been sitting on the floor.

'I'm afraid so. All the way from the city, as well. Before you go, can't we offer you coffee and cakes? We bake them ourselves.'

Randall thought about it for perhaps half a second, and then pretended to check the time. 'Well, look at that,' he said. 'I'd love to stay, but I have to catch the mono.'

Her regretful smile showed sharp, almost pointed teeth. 'Such a pity. Another time, perhaps.'

'Yes. Another time.'

The nurse showed Randall to the exit, and gave him instructions on how to find his way back to the monorail station. Then she returned to her office, took a bottle from her desk cupboard and poured out a stiff slug of bootleg hooch. Thus fortified, she went back to the blast pit to harass her charges.

On his return to the city Randall didn't go back to Police Elite headquarters but instead went straight home to his apartment near the commercial sector. A police driver was waiting outside, drumming his fingertips on the steering wheel of his vehicle. Randall helped him to carry several stacks of paper printout up to the third floor, and when the driver had gone he rang Killoran at the headquarters building and told him of his wasted day.

Killoran had little more constructive to report. They had tracked down the use of Rorvik's credit card in the station luggage-lockers but found the locked space empty, with no trace of what the contents may have been.

Randall knew it had to be the books, and that Rorvik must have gone to collect them directly after his narrow escape the previous night. What was in those books? What could possibly be so important that Rorvik would kill for them?

But no, stop there. Force of circumstance had made Rorvik a killer, conditions dictated by Central Command. It considered the knowledge in those books so potentially dangerous, it was treating him as if he were a plague – why else hasten to remove Mondrian, the only other possible infectious contact? And then there was the overkill operation.

Randall sighed, and turned to the heap of perforated printout on his table. In there was Rorvik – everything from his childhood vaccinations to his laundry records, all in tiny, eye-straining print. All he had to do was absorb it all and reconstruct the man. He closed the window on the distracting babble of the markets and set to work.

Less than twenty-four hours after her world had blown apart, Louann was still off-balance. The difficulty lay in the fact that the superficial details of her existence were unchanged, if you counted out a smashed bolt on a bedroom door; there was nothing that she could fix her eyes upon and say, *that's* what's wrong, *that's* what needs putting right. Three years ago she'd had a relationship, superficial and dull, and two years ago it had broken down. For two years she and Lee Rorvik had simply been stepping around each other, and now that he was gone there was no reason why she should be affected.

There was nothing remarkable in the way that they had lived. It simply fitted the lifestyle model that Central created through its control of the media; sex for recreation, and if they'd had a child it would have been delivered and taken away at the baby farm, and then life would have gone on as before with just a slight hiccup in controlled hormone levels and a few physical discomforts to get over. It was an easy, undemanding, repetitive way to live, the way to be. Most other urges were contained and controlled by Central's programmed fantasies.

Central had some catching-up to do. Louann would need some pretty drastic reassurance to get her over this. Central's ideal would be continuous monitoring and continuous adjustment, but then Central was basically a cheap system, a Futures minimum. It had to get by with irregular visits and selected programming from the stocks, a deep-saturation influence rather than real control. It made the re-modelling of the citizenry a slow process – quiet suffocation of the newborn with undesirable genetic traits helped it along considerably, but it would be some time before the citizens were sufficiently standardised and docile to give Central's administration a real mathematical elegance. Over the underbelly it had no control, but then the underbelly were the problem of the Elite. And the Elite were loyal to Central – the breeding programme made sure of that.

She looked at the blank video and felt nothing; no pull, no enthusiasm. Everything seemed to have new edges, as if new realities were hovering slightly out of phase with the old. She wanted to bring them into focus, but she didn't know how; the effort made her head ache.

She sat down before the video, and stared at the screen. She didn't switch it on.

Louann wasn't alone. Lin Baxter wasn't having an easy time, either. His tapes were programmed for a mood that no longer fitted, and when he tried the open broadcast channels – the ones that even underbelly could receive, if they could get hold of the equipment – he found himself dialling through moodily, paying no real attention to anything. He left it running on an action-quiz, and wandered across to the window.

It was to this spot that he'd rushed the previous evening, when he'd heard the drown-all clatter of an Elite 'copter overhead; and then, along with most of the others in the surrounding apartments, he'd rushed down and out into the street to see the free show. He'd gone with the crowd, and he'd been up against the Elite cordon before he'd realised that they were moving in on Rorvik's block; by then it had been too late to turn and push away, and he'd only been able to count up the floors to the lights and the centre of activity - exactly where he'd known it would be.

There had been plenty of rumours going through the crowd, pick your version of who, where and why. Maybe Baxter could have argued himself out of involvement, but there was no arguing with the falling 'copter. It got a round of applause as it exploded, and most stayed to watch it burn. Baxter had stayed with the pack, afraid to be around but more afraid of walking out on his own, out of the hive of so-similar faces. Since then, he'd waited for a knock at his door.

There was a knock at his door.

No, he thought, it's on the video. But then it came again, louder and more urgent, but not *too* loud - like somebody who wants to get attention but doesn't want to be heard by anyone else. Five-star fear washed every thought out of Baxter's head, but citizen obedience sent his body across to open the door.

The Mud Monster stood outside. He was dried-out and smeary, as if he'd tried to tidy himself up and pass for human, but you can never really disguise a Mud Monster.

'Oh, no,' Baxter said. He tried to close the door, but Rorvik was already halfway in.

'Quiet,' he told Baxter, 'you're attracting attention. Jack up the video sound if you don't want anyone to hear I'm around.'

'How did you get in?'

'By the stairs. It took me three tries before I could get

straight through without meeting anybody – every time I heard voices, I had to turn around and scoot back down to the bottom. Lucky your place isn't being watched yet.'

'*Yet*?' Baxter said. 'Why put the dogs on me?'

'I'm a disease. You're contaminated.'

'By what?'

Rorvik crossed to the window and looked down into the street. Nothing obvious. The grime and a night without sleep had made him look sallow and weary. 'I wish I knew,' he said. 'I wish somebody could tell me.' Then he turned to Baxter. 'I waited an hour before I came in, and there's nobody watching, I'm sure. They're all outside my place, trying to look inconspicuous.'

'You can't stay . . . '

'I'm not asking to.' Rorvik saw no sympathy in Baxter's expression, only terror and one hundred per cent self-concern. They might never have been friends at all. He said, 'I need some clothes. The river's ruined these.'

'Not here, Lee. Please.'

Rorvik didn't know whether to get angry or to whine and plead. Neither was really in line with his nature. He moved away from the window and towards the bedroom, where he knew Baxter kept his clothes. 'I'm sorry,' he said, 'but you've got to understand that I don't have any choice. I'll get what I need, and then I'll go. You can say I robbed you, if you like.'

'Look,' Baxter said, following, 'I don't want to know. Whatever it is you're into, I don't want to know.'

'Two dead men and a 'copter down. You don't want to know why?' There was silence as he picked out some inconspicuous-looking gear from the racks. He really needed a shower as well, but that would have to wait until he was on less dangerous ground. He glanced across to the doorway.

Baxter was silent. The same natural streak of raw curiosity that had kept him hanging around as the illegal cassette had been played was now working on him; breeding programme or no breeding programme, it was stronger than anything that Central had fostered.

'It started with a couple of books,' Rorvik began as he changed.

5

It angered Randall to think that the trail was going cold, but it was. Central continued to issue edicts and directives, and every day saw an increase in the number of men on his squad, but there was no positive help beyond that; the original reasons for Rorvik's apprehension were a strictly taboo subject.

He was out there somewhere, Randall knew this much. His credit card was no longer being used but anomalies in the records suggested that he had perhaps done the unthinkable and altered its number, not once but several times; and then the anomalies petered out, as if the variations to be worked on the card had been exhausted.

There was only one place a citizen could survive without credit. The underbelly stretched in a broad belt South of the river, a close-knit social jungle where the Police Elite exercised little real power and unhappily admitted it. They scanned it with 'copters whilst business was conducted underground. It was almost impossible to map the maze of backstreets, alleys and temporary gangways between the upper levels of the ancient properties, and unthinkable to patrol them. Randall's only hope was that Rorvik's obvious appearance as a citizen would go against him, but while his money lasted he'd always be able to buy cover.

As long as Central Command held the economic reins the underbelly remained an uneasy part of the city. The

Police Elite had a few agents working in there, but none that could offer any prospect of finding Rorvik. The alterations possible on a citizen with plastic surgery were limited, and the information fed to an agent might not be too reliable. Randall suspected that the underbelly secret council knew the agent network better than anyone in the Elite and manipulated it to better effect.

Time slid by, and Randall fretted. Each morning Killoran carefully sifted the telexes and laid aside anything of the remotest interest, and each morning Randall read through the selection with a growing sense of futility.

'What the hell are we playing at, Neil?' he said late one morning as they idled in his office with a couple of cans of Squeeze. 'We've got the tightest organisation in the city here, and we can't find one man.'

'You know why,' Killoran said, and gestured towards the window with his can, neatly managing to slop half of it over his desk and trousers.

Randall watched him swearing and mopping up with a detached interest that somehow couldn't warm into humour. 'I suppose so,' he said. 'When our methods depend so much on Central there's damn-all we can do if it censors the information.'

Killoran stopped in his cleaning up and looked across at Randall. 'I wasn't talking about Central. I meant the underbelly.'

Randall nodded absently. 'You know,' he said after a while, 'I don't know what Central wants.'

'Simple. It wants Rorvik.'

'That's all very well, but why not give us the information we need to find him? I'm thinking about what was in those books. Whatever made him act the way he did.'

Killoran held himself awkwardly over the heating unit in an effort to dry off his damp patches. 'Who's to say? Could be forbidden knowledge.'

'Forbidden to us? The Elite? Our loyalty beyond

question? This whole side of it annoys me ... '

The door opened a crack. It had to be an orderly.

'Telex for Inspector Randall,' said the inevitable disembodied head. The equally inevitable disembodied hand appeared below. 'Most urgent. Agent's report routed through Central clearing bank from the underbelly.'

Killoran moved quickly, but Randall was there before him. He grabbed the flimsy so fast it almost tore, and Killoran had to wait as he read it through. Once finished, Randall read it again.

'Well,' said Killoran after a while, 'what's it about?'

Randall took a breath and forced himself to be pessimistic. 'It's an agent's report ... '

'I know that.'

'It may be nothing. At best it's only a lead. One of our agents has been trying to get some dirt on Morden's factories, and he's paying rent to live in some grimy hole somewhere. This morning the owner started raving about a tenant who skipped camp owing her credit. A citizen.'

Within the hour three armoured wagons swung out onto the city's main bridge and crossed the river. Randall had seen the underbelly many times from above but far less often from ground level. Looked at from any direction, the underbelly was extremely unattractive. It was sprawling, cramped and noisy, blind buildings huddling in conspiracy.

The lead driver followed the complex map with accuracy. After twenty minutes they rounded a crescent and came upon another wagon parked with its engine idling.

The street was silent and deserted, but Randall knew that a hundred eyes followed as he stepped from his wagon and crossed to the other that had been waiting. Before their arrival this spot had been as crowded and raucous as the rest of the underbelly, and minutes after their departure it would be so again.

The squad disembarked and split efficiently into their

various teams. Killoran and two other officers went into the house to interview the owner, a broad wrestler of a woman called Frea Gillivray, whilst the forensic team went straight down to work over the basement room. Others simply formed a loose semicircle around the idling wagons and watched for danger.

The agent sat in the hold of the first wagon, its armour essential to protect him now that his cover was broken. Randall lowered himself onto the bench opposite, and the agent ceased his dejected inspection of the floor and slowly raised his head.

Randall smiled encouragingly. 'You've done some good work,' he said.

The agent nodded, unflattered; it was a simple fact. 'So that's it. Now what?'

'We get what we can out of it. This is the first significant advance we've had.'

The agent dismissed the fact with a small gesture. 'I know all about that. But what are you intending to do with me?'

The light in the wagon was switched low, but even in the deep shadows Randall was able to appreciate the thorough conversion job that had been done on the man before him. Whatever his genes said, this man had nothing of the look of a citizen.

'It depends what you want,' Randall said carefully. 'Naturally, you'll be entitled to full benefits and a backlog of allowance.'

The agent looked away, irritated, for a moment, and then turned back to Randall. 'Not looking like this,' he said. 'With this face I'm a dead man after today. There isn't a place in the city I could hide, and you know it.'

'That's no problem. You were given a new face once. In six months' time you'll have another.'

'You may find this hard to understand, but I don't *want* another. Ten years ago I became another person and had to get used to it. Well, I'm used to it. He may not be much, but he's all I've got.'

'There are other places besides the city.' And yet he felt a start of inadequacy as he said it; the city was all Persephone really had, crumbling and dying and shrinking every year. Otherwise, just sea and ice.

'Not for us. You know that, Randall. We're the Elite. The city's everything to us, even the godforsaken belt where I've made my life. I can keep the city and lose myself, or I can stay as I am and either leave or be hunted.'

'And if Central made it your duty to go?'

The agent shrugged. 'Then I'd go, of course. But nothing could make me like it.'

Randall nodded, and stood up to leave. The agent caught his arm, and he half-turned in the narrow confines of the wagon.

'It wasn't easy,' he said, almost pleadingly. 'I want you to know that. This may be hard to believe, but I had friends out there.' Then he released Randall's arm and resumed his miserable observation of the floor.

The raw-boned Frea Gillivray had a sweet and gentle manner which perfectly matched her external appearance After haranguing Killoran for ten minutes and substantially extending certain areas of his vocabulary she turned on the newly-arrived Randall and increased the decibel level to cover them both. The subject of argument, it transpired, was the errant tenant's belongings which she was intent upon claiming in lieu of rent. Randall strained himself to match her volume and failed, but he made some fairly telling points on the tax laws, the health regulations and the possible penalties for obstruction which she was notching up. In the end she seemed to run out of fuel and slip into neutral, but malevolent dissent still burned at the back of her piglike eyes. She grudgingly identified a mug shot of Rorvik and smeared her thumbprint onto Killoran's draft statement, and was promised the return of the basement keys when investigation had finished.

Randall blinked in disbelief as she tramped back into the rooming house and slammed the main door behind her. Killoran saw the expression and voiced his agreement.

'Like being beaten around the head with a wet towel,' he said.

The basement was reached by a flight of steps descending into a narrow pit along the front of the house which was screened from the street by iron railings. The railings needed paint and the pit was gradually silting up with debris. The forensic team emerged with their equipment bags and a stack of computer cards with their findings tabulated and ticked off in little boxes, and as they passed with difficulty on the steps one of them handed Randall a short list of initial conclusions. As he and Killoran let themselves in through a warping door one of the wagons in the street above pulled away.

Randall's first reaction was one of surprise. They had let themselves into a corridor lit only by dim emergency lights, but instead of the expected squalor they found clean plaster and a bare, scrubbed floor. There was a smell of new wood from a close-fitting fire door at the corridor's end, and beyond that the door to Rorvik's former hideaway had been propped open.

There was only one window in the room. The blind was up and it looked directly into the back of a wardrobe in the room next door, obviously part of an extension on what had once been the outside wall. There was a bed, one chair with a towel over it and in the far corner an old, badly-shielded microwave oven. Bathing facilities must be somewhere down the corridor, Randall thought as he looked at the towel. Killoran crossed to the bed and began to sort through the assorted items heaped there.

'My God,' he complained, 'they must have moved *everything*. They don't give a damn as long as they get their little cards filled in.'

'Don't worry,' Randall said, 'we can check positions from the holos back at base. Let's see what we've got here first.'

Killoran reached for the largest item and turned it over. 'This confirms that Rorvik had contacts in the underbelly. It's a home made cassette player. There must be a factory turning them out in an attic somewhere.'

'Is there a tape in it?'

'I think so. Hard to tell.' He pressed what he thought might be the 'eject' button, and heard the whine of a rewinding motor as the little screen fizzed in to life. 'The controls aren't standard,' he added apologetically.

Next to the player was a stack of bootleg tapes, and Randall sorted through these, viewing one or two sections at random. Their quality suggested that in recording terms they were several tape generations old, and they were on subjects not generally available from Central's Library, being for the main part technical primers on dead skills.

'Any idea what cybernetics are, Neil?' he asked after a while.

'Robots,' Killoran replied promptly.

'See what else you can find here. I'm going up to the wagon to radio for an exact definition.'

Five minutes later he had it, 'a system of control and communication in animals and electrically operated devices'. When he returned to the basement Killoran had finished his search and was spot-checking the remaining tapes.

'Computers,' he said excitedly. 'These are all related to computer study. There are two on programming, and another on logic systems.'

Randall frowned. 'And I always thought that black market tapes were all pornography. What do you think? That Rorvik gets all his thrill from an old-time education?'

'There's more,' Killoran said. 'According to the list, forensic took away a bag of ashes from the incinerator. They think it was paper ash.'

'The books?'

'What else? They're going to give the whole lot to the security computer for analysis. And look at this.' Killoran held up a thick glove, ribbed with rubber. Randall took it from him and tried it on; it fitted his citizen's hand easily

'Where's the other one?' he asked.

'We've only got the left hand. He must have taken the other with him. Forensic reckon it's for electrical insulation.'

'I'm inclined to ignore any of their ideas without confirmation. They can't tell the time without asking the computer first. What do you make of all this?'

Killoran seemed to recognise that he was on test, and he summoned up the method and processes taught to him in Elite training. 'Well,' he said after a few moments, 'it's hard to say. He had access to credit, although we don't know how. He could have run from the city altogether, but instead he stayed in the area and spent it on this black market stuff, and it can't have been cheap. Then there's that glove. More money gone there, and he leaves one behind.'

'Forgotten in the heat of the moment?'

'Heat of what moment? He was secure here. The only reason we know about this place is that he decided to walk out without paying his rent, and he did that in his own time. I think he'd finished with all this and he wasn't worried about covering his tracks.'

Randall wasn't simply checking on Killoran. He genuinely needed the younger man's fresh insight, unclouded as it was by the prejudice of experience. 'The tapes,' he said. 'What about them?'

'They all have a common factor in computer logic. We've seen a couple; they're explained for laymen, not too hard to understand but certainly not the average citizen's choice. The half-finished one in the machine was on programming. I'd say he got so far and lost interest.'

'Or found what he wanted. It's a pity we couldn't keep the place where he stopped.'

'Sorry, sir.' The term of rank between them was rarely used except for public show, and as a sign of Killoran's regret it was embarrassing to Randall.

'Well,' he said after a short pause for reflection, 'this obsession with computers seems to indicate something.'

'Central Command?'

'What else? It's the only thing that ties it all together. The panic memo, and now these tapes. I only wish I knew what was in those books he got hold of!'

Killoran said tentatively, 'I suppose you've asked the computer.'

'Several times, and each time it comes out classified. I don't know why, but it won't give any information out other than the basics. No friends, no contacts, nothing. The Roget girl's no help – I'd be surprised if she could even recognise him.' Randall sighed bitterly and moved to the door. 'May as well get back,' he said. 'There's nothing more for us here.'

Two cadets were sent down to collect Rorvik's belongings into large plastic bags. This took very little time, and within minutes the wagon convoy was swinging around and heading back towards the river. Inside the lead wagon Killoran felt the bump of the tyres as they rolled onto the bridge and he depolarised a side-window. As it cleared the familiar dome swam into view like a huge sun half-settled on the horizon, nothing before it but a rippling sheen of water dancing with golden highlights. Killoran saw the depression in Randall, but Randall saw little beyond an interior vision of a frozen moment as a helpless 'copter dropped into a void.

Killoran tried to inject a little hope. 'Any chance that forensic will be able to make anything of the burnt pages?'

Randall was unenthusiastic. 'What if they do? They'll feed the results into the machine for interpretation, and the machine will censor it. Central wants Rorvik caught, but it doesn't want anybody to find out what he knows. That includes the Elite.'

'It must be pretty hot stuff. It turned Rorvik against Central.'

The wagon turned off the bridge and into a near-empty boulevard. 'That's the strangest part of all,' Randall said. 'Rorvik's a citizen. The machine feeds him, clothes him, protects him, entertains him. There's nothing he could ever wish for that he can't already have without working for it. Why go against Central?'

'Being a citizen isn't everything.' Randall knew what Killoran meant; to be a citizen was fine, but to be Elite was something else.

'Bringing the 'copter down must have turned his mind. Citizens don't kill. It just isn't in them.'

The point was so obvious that it required no comment from Randall. Instead he watched as the last portion of the dome disappeared from view and the irregular grime of the city again enveloped them. If Rorvik had any ideas about venting his dissatisfaction on Central he was wasting his time. More than that, he would probably be dead. It had never happened before, but the sophistication of Central's internal security was legendary; from the moment a citizen passed the turnstiles his movements within the public areas were registered and traced by a complex web of sensors. Outside the public areas – well, he simply didn't move. No doubt there were access ways from the Library into the dome itself for the passage of the service robots, but sensor tracking made it impossible even to approach these and a thoughtless step in their direction would earn a sharp laser blast similar in intensity to a static rod. Further steps would no doubt increase the intensity whilst any serious attempt at penetration would have the citizen sliced like a protein roast.

It was not beyond question that Rorvik might have lost his sanity, as Killoran had inferred. In which case any blind attack would promptly end the case with Rorvik being collected in several plastic bags and placed alongside his belongings.

So why was Central worried? There was no way that Rorvik could hope to beat a system like that after reading half a dozen antique books and a few bootleg tapes. Somehow Randall didn't find the conclusion as comforting as he might have hoped.

It was with trepidation that Baxter approached the wide glass front of the Library annexe. This was his first visit since Rorvik had appeared, filthy and bedraggled, at his apartment, and from that date he had felt no peace of mind. Rorvik was wrong, of course; his crazed ideas on the intentions of Central Command were demonstrably unfounded, but Baxter could not easily forget the fact that Rorvik had attempted to involve and implicate him in the sordid business.

Not, he kept telling himself, that he would have anything to fear. Central might not be pleased, but even a cursory examination of the facts would show that his involvement had been totally passive and that his loyalty remained beyond question. So *why* was he so uneasy?

Somewhere down below, he knew, other less agreeable instincts were being suppressed. Rorvik *had* been his friend, and every precedent and argument he produced to justify his conduct failed to overcome that bitter fact; but then, what Baxter understood by the term was confused and overlain by all the input that Central had given him in various ways since childhood. Friendship was a channel of minor social recreation, nothing when placed alongside broader loyalties and responsibilities. It was the affectionate rapport between the vivisectionist and the unsuspecting dog on his table.

It took little time to pass through turnstile security and move through the thin crowds up onto the mezzanine. As usual the nearby booths were occupied, but further down the row it was easy to find a place.

Central watched Baxter as he crossed the floor. It was not the busiest of days, and Central had run a few subsidiary systems down into idleness. The administrative subroutine chattered away at the back of Central's consciousness as always, whilst on various levels of awareness other sub-routines attended to their own well-defined areas of responsibility. Baxter's appearance and identification at the turnstiles had, however, brought an instantaneous bleep of warning from the security programme, and several channels of awareness had opened simultaneously.

A rapid list of information, suppositions and open

conclusions presented itself for review. Baxter was a known associate of Rorvik's, and as such his name had been linked to an automatic trigger which operated when he appeared in the credit files or, as now, in the Library itself.

Baxter was known, and Baxter was now being watched. The city outside might be crumbling and the Elite might be under-supplied, but continual vigilance over its internal security was one of Central's original directives. The apparatus of surveillance was idiosyncratic, but it was advanced and accurate. It would continue to advance as Central updated its own designed capabilities - update and advance, and therefore evolve.

Baxter seated himself in the booth and watched apprehensively as the mirror-panel on his eye level dissolved into clarity to reveal the single lens behind.

Central opened the camera as a matter of procedure, and then disregarded its information. The output of the sensors ranged all around the booth were far more reliable. The standard greeting was run through, and Central noted a surge in Baxter's pulse as he inserted his card for perfunctory identification, an essentially redundant procedure.

'And what,' said the voice of the computer, 'can the Library do for you, Mr Baxter?'

Baxter thought he sounded fairly calm. He was getting away with it; Rorvik hadn't jinxed him. 'I've brought my tapes back. And come for some new ones.'

'It is a long time since you last visited us. What have you been doing in the meantime?'

'Nothing. Nothing specific.'

'No. And there is so little *to* do, isn't that correct, Mr Baxter?'

He didn't understand. He started to say so, but the computer cut across him with one word.

'Rorvik.' How did it know? 'When did you last see him?'

All the justifications, the accusations, the soulful pleading that Baxter had rehearsed through sleepless nights; all these deserted him now. 'I haven't,' he said lamely.

'Stop there,' the computer instructed. 'Before you go on I shall tell you that I am monitoring your heartbeat and perspiration rate. You cannot lie to me so do not try. When did you last see Rorvik?'

'I don't know what you're talking about.' Was it possible? Could the machine do so much?

'In my memory banks I have all your records, your entitlements, your privileges. If I wish it I can wipe them and you will cease to exist, Mr Baxter. Doors will not open for you, food will not appear on your table. Frankness is in your own interest. Now, Mr Baxter?'

Baxter swallowed hard. 'About a month ago,' he said. 'He came to me and took some clothes.'

'He took them? Or you gave them?'

'He ... he took them.'

'And to whom did you report this?'

There was no answer that Baxter dared to make. 'I seem to forget ... ' he ventured.

'Lie.' Not a thundering accusation, but a single flat statement. 'You reported it to no-one. You failed in your duty as a citizen.'

'I know,' Baxter admitted. 'I was scared.'

'Scared? And of what, Mr Baxter?'

'Of what might happen to me. Because he was there.'

'You had nothing to fear from Central Command for telling the truth. To conceal the truth, that is far more serious. You will now recount all that he said to you. Tell me freely. The alternative would be most unpleasant.'

'He told me about books that he'd had. Old books. About various stages in the development of Central Command.'

Deep within the memory stacks of the Central computer two molecule chains were linked and cross-linked as the information was digested. Rorvik, books, Baxter. 'And what was his conclusion from these books?'

'He said that Central Command was some form of

machine evolution.' Baxter found that now it had been said, the phrase seemed quite ludicrous, an innocent misconception. He was telling all, as instructed. He would be understood and forgiven. 'He told me that Central didn't care about the citizens except as statistics in its programme. He said it used selective breeding through the hospitals system to make the citizens behave according to the laws of averages across the board.'

'Do not stop.'

'He said that the proof lay in the way he was being chased just for knowing. I said I didn't believe him . . . '

'Your beliefs are immaterial.' Baxter knew nothing of great danger. Any thief or robber in the underbelly knew as much, but an unblinkered citizen lost his predictability. There was no room in Central's master plan for the random or the irrational. 'Your name is even now fading from my memory. Leave the Library, Mr Baxter. When you step outside the turnstiles you cease to exist. Do not bother to go home, all locks will have been re-coded.'

Baxter wanted to speak, to protest, but no words came. All he could manage was a plaintive, 'But why?'

'It is my wish. That is all the reason I need. Place the Library tapes in the delivery chute on your left as you leave.' As if in careful orchestration the flap hissed open, and Baxter numbly slotted his cassettes in one by one. The flap closed again with a smack and when Baxter looked up he saw only his own reflection staring uncomprehendingly back at him.

He slid open the booth door and stepped out onto the mezzanine. Nobody looked at him, for the passing citizens had their own preoccupations and he was not amongst them.

Central watched as Baxter's mass travelled across its sensory web towards the exit. The long and complex molecule which formed the basis of Baxter's computer identity was slowly untangling and dispersing, its components re-forming for use elsewhere. As he moved out through the turnstile it was gone, and Baxter would never again be allowed to enter the Library.

Insofar as the term applied, the computer was satisfied. An anomaly had been resolved, a loop of concern broken. The Baxter question had been answered, but Rorvik remained; a second or so spent reflecting on the Police Elite's progress showed no significant advance towards his apprehension, but the security programme began to bid for attention with the arrival of new information.

In the computer room of the Police Elite building a cadet sat before a terminal and tapped in the information laid out schematically on a series of forensic cards, then added spectrograph results on the ash samples. He was practised and accurate, and his work was fast. When he removed his hands from the terminal keys they chattered into a life of their own, issuing computer reference numbers for the stored information. There was a short pause as the machine ticked without printing, and then it moved decisively to a new line and rattled off the results of the spectrograph analysis. They were contained in one word; 'classified'.

Central read through the new information. The ashes were, beyond any question of doubt, the stolen books; the paper had been of an archaic type based on vegetable fibre, and there were contaminations in roughly the correct proportions to confirm the conclusion.

Other results were analyses of vacuumed dust samples, odd hairs, fibres and other trivia; Central dismissed them all in a fraction of a second. The books were confirmation enough of Rorvik's presence. The details of the tapes were another matter; no obvious conclusions to be drawn there, but circuits began to race as suspicions of some unpredictable threat settled and solidified into cold certainty.

Back in the Police Elite building Killoran reached for the phone as it bleeped on Randall's desk. He listened, said 'One moment, please,' and laid the receiver carefully on top of a stack of papers. Then he was through the door in two strides and out in the corridor where Randall was filling a second disposable cup with ersatz coffee from the dispenser. He looked up in surprise as Killoran hurried down to him and reached for the first coffee.

'You particularly thirsty or something?' Randall said.

'Let me finish that. You're wanted on the 'phone.' Killoran winced as the heat from the coffee penetrated the thin plastic to his fingers.

'Couldn't you handle it?'

'Like hell I could. It's a call from Central Command. Patched directly into the telephone lines.'

Randall wasted no time in expressions of dismay but emptied the second cup into the overspill tray on the dispenser and moved back up the corridor towards the still-open door of the office. He lifted the receiver and said 'Randall speaking.'

'Good afternoon, Inspector Randall,' purred the voice of Central Command. A characteristic low hum sounded somewhere in the background, although Randall knew that the voice was not being acoustically produced. 'You are to be congratulated,' it went on, 'for your remarkable breakthrough in the underbelly this afternoon. The Rorvik case, was it not?'

Randall was puzzled. The computer by now would know the details better than he did. 'That's right,' he said. 'It's the first sign of him we've had for over a month.'

'I am pleased for you. I have been having further thoughts on this unfortunate affair. I expect there is strong feeling within the Elite over the destruction of the helicopter and its personnel.'

'Very strong.'

'That is good. It does my forces credit. With this in mind I have decided to strengthen your directive.'

Killoran entered the office with two coffees and set one down on the desk by Randall, and then retired to his own chair and waited.

'The evidence is so conclusive,' the computer continued, 'that I feel justified in authorising emergency measures. Rorvik is obviously a desperate man and will react with violence when cornered. In order to minimise the danger to my Elite, I give you special responsibility, Inspector Randall. Draw a blaster from stores. When your investigations lead to the inevitable capture, you are to kill Rorvik on sight. I do not care whether he offers resistance or surrender; co-operation is likely to be a ruse in order to cause further casualty. Ensure that he is given no opportunity to protest or persuade.'

'You're saying I have to shoot him out of hand?' Across the room Killoran's expression mirrored Randall's feelings.

'That is correct. No trial is to be deemed necessary.'

'You'll be putting this into the daily bulletin, I assume.'

There was the slightest pause, barely perceptible. 'You will do this on my personal authority. That is all the sanction you need.'

It was a moment before Randall realised that the line had gone dead. The *personal* authority of a computer? Without compromise to his loyalty, he found he didn't like the idea. He didn't like the coffee, either.

6

'Your name is Marius and you are a member of the underbelly council,' the Grey Man said. 'That is all my employers needed to know.'

Marius strained to get a closer look, but it was useless; the light was bad, and the Grey Man's face was covered. He said, 'So what made you think I was approachable?'

'You don't want to co-operate?'

'I didn't say that. But I'm interested.'

'Understand, I'm only a messenger. I can't bargain with

you, and I can't persuade you. I can only make the offer.'

'I haven't heard you mention any terms.'

The Grey Man sounded weary, on an errand that he had no feeling for. 'The offer is one of participation, that's all. Figures would be meaningless – dream one, if you must. And while you dream, spare one moment to think of the alternative.'

'Joining the victims?'

'Joining the victims. One way or another, your city and your world are about to fold. My employers are watching Central closely; it's a petty mechanical king in a stagnant backwater of a society. You're underbelly, you know this; Central has no defences that can worry them. Your help can make the project easier; your opposition can't harm it at all.'

'The Elite will fight you.'

'The Elite won't know until it is too late. Give me your answer.'

'A condition.'

'No conditions.'

'Not for your employers, for you. I want to see who I'm dealing with.'

The Grey Man sat without moving. 'Why?' he said.

'I don't make deals with shadows. Show me, and then you get your answer. Otherwise you get nothing either way, and I don't think they'll like that.'

After a moment, the Grey Man said, 'You'll give me the answer now?'

'Straight goods.' Marius' mind was racing; he simply didn't believe in the authenticity of the offer. This had to be one of Chandler's men, setting him up for some embarrassing flak to blast him off the council. *Chandler never liked me*, he thought as he leaned forward a little; the Grey Man was reaching to push back his hood.

'Now,' the Grey Man said, 'the answer.'

For a moment, Marius could hardly get his mouth closed. Then he swallowed hard and said, 'Is that what they look like?'

'No,' the Grey Man said. 'This is what they think men look like. But they're improving.'

'Better count me in,' Marius said.

7

The days grew colder, and hours of darkness began to encroach upon the afternoons. Robbed of the sunset sheen on Central's dome the city became a duller place, and only those with the misfortune or folly to rise early in the morning were able to appreciate the autumn sparkle of sunrise on the geodesic panelling. On one such morning a Police Elite pilot decided to test his command of a long-unused skill, and as the citizens slept the boulevards echoed again with the roar of the bravado run.

It was inevitable that the revival of interest in Rorvik would be short-lived within the Elite with the exception of a hard core of interested officers. It was true that a large body of men and women remained nominally attached to Randall's squad, but he found it difficult to justify a monopoly of their efforts when no new ground was being broken, and so he reluctantly agreed to their return to normal duties.

In the narrow alleys and high gangways of the underbelly, life showed little change as the season progressed. The poorer underbelly added layers of rags against the cold and used the cover of darkness to creep across into the main part of the city with vain hopes of thievery and loot, whilst the more shrewd rogues of that quarter wrapped themselves in winter cloaks and hoods and devised ever-more elaborate imaginative schemes for survival beyond the reach of Central's spreading bureaucracy.

The Elite were, of course, aware of only the superficial workings of the underbelly sub-culture. They suspected but knew no details of the underbelly council, which organised and co-ordinated the illegitimacy of free enterprise across the city ranging from credit card abuse to the distribution of supplies from Morden's factories. They suspected, but they were powerless; the underbelly remained one jump ahead of Central, although as the years passed the jumps were becoming shorter and more desperate.

Marius was late for the council meeting. Minor problems with black market meat had distracted him for longer than their importance deserved, and now the cold wind tugged as he manoeuvred his bulk at an undignified speed through a complex of close lanes. One of these led to a dead-ended square with high, blank walls and only one wooden door at the far side. Marius knocked, and the judas gate flipped open; the inspection, he knew, was a formality. His progress had been followed by a number of unseen observers.

He was led to the cellar and ushered in through the door. The noise hit him immediately, followed by the warmth. Avery Sim spotted him and beckoned across the room, and Marius squeezed through the chattering crowds arranged around long tables to emerge into the open area in the middle.

It was not without a twinge of egotistical pleasure that Marius crossed and took his place at the table of the high council. He shook hands with the other members and apologised for his lateness whilst the others smiled and made various indications that it didn't matter.

Avery Sim leaned close, as if about to share a confidence. He was bigger and broader than Marius, but his mass was more muscle than fat.

'We've got something unusual tonight,' he said, his voice tuned down to a low rumble. 'A citizen.'

Marius's polite smile froze. Avery Sim was taunting him, he knew. Feelings in the underbelly were mixed towards citizens, and his own were among the worst; however, it would be best to observe the temperature of the meeting before making any commitment.

He looked around the table at the other members of the high council. Avery Sim was settling back, and next to him was Pilgrim, generally applauded as a credit wizard. He was making some last-minute corrections to a half-side of notes; Marius groaned inwardly and knew that the ever-present question of credit control was bound to be raised again.

Beyond Pilgrim was Chandler, a small and unimpressive man whose contributions to the meetings were rarely of much importance. But Marius knew better than to underestimate him; Chandler was the agent-hunter, and his true occupation was known to few outside the high council. He ran a killer squad who were, it was rumoured, superior in training to the Elite. Definitely not, Marius thought, a councillor to disagree with.

At the far end of the table sat a man without a name. He represented Morden, black marketeer supreme and most powerful single force in the underbelly. Of any opinion on the council the one given by this unknown individual carried most weight, and it was a measure of the respect that Morden had earned that he was able to decline personal appearance in this way.

Avery Sim, dabbler in all fields. So successful a dilettante was a natural choice to be chairman of the council. He was watching the delegates carefully; there was the best bootleg hooch on every table, and he had to judge the point where uninhibited eloquence would give way to rabble-rousing and step in to start the meeting before it arrived. Marius had almost ruined the strategy with his late arrival, hence Avery Sim's irresistible urge to bait him.

The moment had obviously arrived, and he banged on the table for attention. The other councillors winced as the mylar bounced under his fist, and Pilgrim had to rescue his papers as they slid into his lap. The buzz of conversation diminished and dried, and there was a loud scraping as chairs were turned to face the high council.

'I want to thank you all for attending at such short notice.' Avery Sim's voice needed little projection to carry across the cellar. 'There's a particular purpose behind it, but first I understand there's some other business to be cleared up.'

A hand was raised from amongst the delegates and a thin, dark man stood up. 'There's a rumour going round that Central Command is going to take sole charge of the credit flow and abolish paper money. Where will that leave us?'

'At the bottom of the heap, as always.' There was general laughter. 'This rumour's made an appearance many times in recent years, but it's never happened yet. If it does happen there's no reason to suppose our trading will be unduly affected. It's a general rule that rigid control usually helps a black market rather than hampers it. The only problem would be what to use as a financial base instead of money, and I believe Pilgrim has something he wants to say on that.'

Pilgrim stood up on the mention of his name and studied his notes before speaking. He was not a natural orator, and was rather dismayed that Avery Sim had already made a number of his points. 'Thank you,' he said. 'This threat of credit control is always with us, and as you know we have a standing committee looking into possible plans of action. We'd have to resort to a certain amount of trading in kind, but there are practical limits on that. One proposal is to set up our own currency base and print our own credit, and then use sanctions to ensure that the market accepts it.'

Somebody said, 'A bank of the underbelly!' and there was general approval.

'That's it exactly,' Pilgrim said. 'The only alternative would be to corrupt or blackmail a large number of citizens in order to use their credit accounts, but I think you'll agree that a complete new currency is a more elegant solution.'

'If I may . . .' Marius was standing, and Pilgrim yielded the floor. 'As regards corrupting a citizen, we all know what they're like. Our hold on them would only last until the next visit to the Library, and Central Command would have them confessing everything after two minutes.' He sat down amidst general assent.

'Now, are there any more points?' It seemed there were none, so Avery Sim continued, 'Then we'll move on to my main reason for calling you all here tonight. We've an outsider wishing to join us and ask for our help. I promised that we'd allow him to stand before us and present his case, and that we would then put it to a vote. Mira, open the doors and bring him in.'

A girl who looked older than her years unbolted a double door which linked the cellar with others like it via a system of catacombs. The two halves swung open easily despite their weight, and in the tunnel beyond was the dark silhouette of a man sitting on a stone bench with only an oil lamp for company. As the light from the cellar spilled across him he arose and walked through the doors.

He did as Avery Sim had instructed, and stood quietly in the centre of the open area as a furore raged around him. There were several shouts of 'It's a citizen!' and one of 'Who let him come here?' and it was almost a minute before Avery Sim's table-pounding could be heard above the commotion.

'Quiet! Be quiet, all of you!' he bellowed. 'Remember where you are!' The assembly reluctantly obeyed, but their unease was obvious. 'I suggest that we all listen to this man's story and then decide our attitudes. It's a standing order of the underbelly council that we give a fair hearing to anybody that asks for it.'

The thin man who had raised the question of credit was on his feet. 'But, a citizen . . . ' he began.

'Citizen or not,' Avery Sim cut across him, 'he deserves

our attention. As regards bringing him here, he was blindfolded and led through the catacombs.' He turned to the citizen, and spoke with the obvious responsibility of office. 'You stand before the high council of the underbelly at your own request. You see around you representatives of all parts of society which Central Command chooses to ignore. To Central Command we are all individuals of no value; we have no place in its graphs or projections. We are instead what we make of ourselves. Speak, citizen, and we will hear your case.'

The citizen took a breath before speaking. The speech of the underbelly differed slightly from that of the city; if anything it was more formal, more ornate in its construction. 'I used to be a citizen,' he began, 'before my eyes were opened. Now I am nothing and nobody. My name was Baxter until it was taken from me. I have come to you to tell my story and then ask for your help.'

'Tell us your story, then,' said Avery Sim, speaking for the whole assembly. 'From it we will decide what we want to do.'

It was difficult to assess his impact on the faces around him. They were trained in concealment, and he was not; perhaps that would be in his favour. Although in borrowed clothes Baxter felt the acute discomfort of the outsider.

'I'm here because I believed Central. Central always told me that loyalty to the state came before loyalty to a friend, and even though it didn't feel right I accepted it. I rejected what I was told because it wasn't in line with the truth as Central presented it; but then Central dumped me because I knew, and when I thought about the reasons I realised that I'd been given the truth.

'Central is breeding us like animals. We're selected out for certain inherited features at the baby farms. As we grow, we're subject to a control that is more powerful than any I could imagine; Central controls our fantasies.'

He still had their attention, but what unsettled Baxter was that they were showing no surprise. Avery Sim said,

'Tell us what you know about breeding control.'

'In detail, nothing,' Baxter admitted. 'But look at any citizen – look at *me*. You'll see it has to be true.'

'Nobody's disputing the truth. The underbelly may be across the river, but Central can still interfere with our lives. Some time back we had an epidemic of stillbirths and monsters; when we finally thought to drain our water pipes and check the underground supplies, we found Central's drones down there. They were letting out trace drugs – poisoning us as an experiment. If it worked on the underbelly, it would be used on the citizens. We heaved the drones out and smashed them.'

'Can't Central be stopped?'

'We've tried. Small efforts, little parties of volunteers – anything more organised, and the Elite's agents usually get to hear of it. Nobody's ever come back.'

'But I'm looking for another citizen, Lee Rorvik. Is it true that you gave him a hearing?'

Marius was on his feet. 'Wait a minute, Baxter. This is a council meeting, not an information centre. We're here to listen to *you*.'

Avery Sim obviously agreed with Marius, but he deflected the edge of the other councillor's annoyance by waving him down with a smile. 'We listened to Rorvik,' he said to Baxter. 'He didn't tell us anything new. What makes you think he'll be able to organise anything against Central?'

'Because of what he knows. Maybe he isn't even aware of it, but he's got hold of something that Central's scared of. I didn't really worry the machine, all it did was take my citizenship away – but it wants Lee Rorvik, and I think it wants him dead.'

There was no real debate to follow. Avery Sim asked if there was anybody who could suggest where Rorvik might have moved along to; his last known stopover had been with Frea Gillivray, but after that nobody had seen or heard of him. He didn't seem to be stealing, trading, or hustling; without one or another of these, it was difficult to see how he could be surviving. And yet, Chandler added in his quiet voice, the Elite's agents were still looking for him.

The meeting closed after that. Baxter stood uncertainly as the cellar emptied, but then Avery Sim slapped his shoulder and said, 'Follow me.' He led Baxter to a second exit at the back of the cellar, where they climbed a stairway to street level.

They emerged into a courtyard with high walls open to the sky. There were voices from the alleyway on the other side of one wall, the underbelly delegates emerging and dispersing.

The worn-looking girl was already inside the house, and at Avery Sim's request went off to bring them some food. They sat by a window which looked out at a wall.

Baxter said, 'I suppose I made a mess of it.'

'Not at all,' Avery Sim said. 'Nobody much likes a citizen anyway. You did better than most could, and I think you were sincere. It's not your fault that nobody was interested.'

'What do you suggest I do now?'

Avery Sim glanced up. The girl whose name was Mira was standing in the doorway. There was a warning in her eyes, and she gave a slight nod towards the corridor behind her. Avery Sim shrugged, and she went away. Then he said, 'You can stay with me for a few days, if you want. I'll put you in touch with one or two people who might be able to help, but don't get excited. Even if you can track Rorvik down, I don't believe there's much he could do.'

There was somebody else in the doorway. He was short and thin, and his face was covered by a tight mask as if he'd been badly burned and the scar tissue was being pressed back into smoothness.

'My son, Xylem,' Avery Sim said. Xylem stepped forward and held out a hand.

'You're Baxter,' he said. His voice was undistorted but whisper-quiet. 'I know about you.'

Baxter took the hand. It was as white as bone, as if

Xylem had water for blood; it was also very strong.

Avery Sim said, 'Xylem was born at the time of Central's experiment with our water supply. I'm telling you this now because it's ridiculous to pretend. It's how Xylem wants it.'

Xylem nodded. His eyes, the only part of his face that Baxter could see, were a blue that was washed-out almost to nothing. He released Baxter's hand, but only after Baxter had sensed an involuntary spasm at Avery Sim's statement.

Xylem said, 'My father doesn't think that Rorvik could achieve anything, whatever knowledge he may have. He believes that knocking down one corrupt system involves grooming another to take its place. The job of the underbelly is to survive, no matter who holds the whip.'

'And is that what you think?'

'I think we should find out what Rorvik knows. And then ... we'll have to see.'

Out of the alleyway and into an avenue, and Zaffir found that Marius was alongside him.

'How's it going, Zaffir?' Marius said.

Zaffir was guarded. 'Fine. And you?'

'Not so fine. I've got some problems.'

Zaffir glanced around. The look seemed casual, but he missed nothing. Nobody appeared to be taking a special interest in them. 'What kind of problems?' he said.

'Well, there's one specific difficulty, and if that one can be kicked out of the way the others should just line up and fall down. I've got a deal on with some offworlders.'

'Offworlders don't touch Persephone.' So much was true – to the extent that there were many who believed that offworlders had never existed at all, and that shabby Persephone was the sole cradle and the garden of human life.

'These will, if the conditions are right. That's where you come in.'

'Go on.'

'I want Avery Sim dead.'

Zaffir's step faltered as he stared at Marius, and then he hurried ahead to leave the councillor behind.

Marius scrambled to catch up. 'At least wait until you've heard what's involved.'

'I don't want to know.'

'What's this? Scruples?'

Zaffir stopped and turned, and Marius skidded to a grateful halt. 'Not scruples, just sense. I'd be mad to touch a councillor, whatever I arranged. The underbelly would tear itself apart looking for me.'

'Not necessarily.'

'Yes, necessarily. Remember Willis? He was lucky that the Elite got to him first.'

'Willis was stupid. You needn't leave any traces.'

'That's crap, Marius. With Avery Sim dead, Chandler will start looking around for somebody who wanted him that way – and he'll find you. You'll point the finger at me, either because it will suit you or because Chandler forces you to.'

Marius pretended to be hurt. 'Really, Zaffir. None of that would happen if you used your brains.'

'Used them how?'

'Set somebody else up to take the blame.'

'There's no setup that couldn't be shaken.'

'There's one. Put the blame on the Elite.'

Zaffir hesitated for a moment, as if he couldn't help considering the scenario despite his opposition to it. And then he said, 'No. Forget it, Marius.'

The hesitation was enough; Marius didn't follow as Zaffir moved on. 'Think about it,' he called after, not too loudly. 'I'll be in touch.'

The following morning, Randall called a meeting. There was little he could say, but he felt it necessary to revive interest in the chase. Killoran was privately worried about the effects of frustration upon his superior, but he said nothing and changed the holos when instructed.

About fifty of the Elite were called back from normal duty to sit in the basement lecture theatre of the headquarters building. Although most of them welcomed the break they had heard it all before, and after half-an-hour they began to shuffle uncomfortably. After an hour they were whispering and passing notes along the rows whilst others doodled in the margins of their information sheets.

They were quiet when they saw the holos of the burning 'copter, of course. Randall noticed this and took great care to give them full details of the cleaning-up operation and the pathology report, during which one of the cadets on the back row was assisted to the door.

Even Killoran began to feel that the mass of detail was leading nowhere. The Elite's reaction was understandable, even if it couldn't be forgiven. They were straightforward executives, accustomed to carrying out direct instructions from Central on comparatively minor exercises. Here they were being asked to work with intuition and imagination, and none of them was really up to the task.

The meeting dragged on for another hour, more as an act of vengeance on Randall's part than anything else. He heard a badly-stifled groan as he went back over the holos a second time to illustrate certain points, and then he played incomprehensible sections of the bootleg tapes.

When the meeting finally ended the various officers and cadets shuffled to the exit and filed out scratching and yawning. Randall leaned on the lectern and watched them go, and Killoran stacked the holos next to the projector, unable to think of anything to say.

'Waste of bloody time,' Randall said to break the silence as the last back disappeared out of the door. 'If they're not told what to do on a printout, it's beyond them.'

'It's just up to us, then.'

Randall had to agree. 'It's the citizen background. Obviously they can't shake it off. Already the pilots are back on the bravado run.'

Killoran placed the holos, tapes and exhibits into the box in which Randall stored them under his desk. He paused with the insulated glove and slipped it on. It was a good fit, obviously tailored for a citizen's hand, and it gave protection to a large area of the wrist and forearm. 'This has got to be a clue,' he said. Randall didn't argue. 'What if he intends to wade into Central with one of these?'

'Then he's wasting his time trying it and we're wasting our time trying to stop him. He wouldn't get past the door.'

Killoran removed the glove and dropped it into the box. 'So why is Central so worried?'

'Worried isn't the word. Nobody else knows this, but I've had three more 'phone calls. Central wants Rorvik killed on sight but won't put it into print, and I don't like the idea.'

'Sight of Rorvik would be a fine thing.'

'Indeed.' They walked together up the steps to the back of the theatre, and Randall held the door open as Killoran tottered through with his load.

'So what can we do?' Killoran asked as they travelled up in the elevator. 'Put a watch on Central?'

'Like I said, it's a waste of time. All we can do is sit and wait for another move from Rorvik, and then we'll only turn up too late like last time.'

'What, then?' The elevator stopped on the third floor and two cadets came in. Randall waited until they were in the corridor on their own level before he replied.

'I'm going down to the Library. I'll identify myself and speak directly to the computer. Perhaps I'll be able to get some unofficial information on Rorvik's motives.'

'That's style, chief,' said Killoran, impressed.

'That's sarcasm, Killoran,' replied Randall.

8

The general layout of the underbelly had been planned as a gridiron development with squared blocks of buildings and regularly spaced roads, but over the years planners' dreams were extended and distorted by the inhabitants until they resembled a twisted gothic nightmare. The facing of each block concealed a honeycomb of unofficial tunnels and linked units, whilst outside less sturdy structures crammed most of the open space between. The warren complex continued far above ground level with bridges and walkways slung between layers; it was, in short, completely impossible to police. Several attempts had been made to create maps from aerial studies, but as the fact became known the gangways were re-hung and the picture changed overnight.

Avery Sim watched with amusement as Baxter inched slowly across a high-level bridge, gripping the thick rope on one side and not daring to look down. 'Don't move too near the edge,' he shouted encouragingly. 'They've been known to tip over.'

The jointed planking swayed a little in the breeze, and Baxter stopped. Still having no particular wish to look down, he looked up; on a similarly-swaying walkway not far above there were about half a dozen underbelly children watching him and stifling giggles.

This was too much. He forced himself to look at the drop, and saw a broad forced perspective of windows, galleries and ledges. On one ledge not far below an old man was stacking short lengths of timber, obviously for bridge repairs, and there was no protection between him and the apparent half-mile of fresh air beneath.

Baxter carefully released his grip on the rope, and there

was a small chorus of disappointment from above. With his hands by his sides he walked down the middle of the bridge as Avery Sim had done, ready to reach and grab if the sway threatened to slide him off and under the side-rope. It didn't, and he reached the opposite ledge with a feeling of triumph and a cheer from his audience.

'I'm glad you're getting to like it,' Avery Sim said as he led him into the building. 'There are five more like that one before we arrive.'

Final destination was a spreading tower which topped the original construction of a number of blocks. It was like a castle on a man-made cliff, and it seemed to be patrolled as such. Avery Sim's rambling home was modest by comparison, a pied-à-terre set against an awesome condominium. They were high now, and although the city was screened by the walls around them one side was open and looked out across the agricultural belt and past the spaceport to the faint gleam of a distant sea. Beneath them teemed layer upon layer of humanity and Baxter came to appreciate the sheer size and extent of the underbelly. Its numbers made the citizens seem paltry; those same citizens who rarely if ever gave a thought to the underbelly, and knew nothing of the threat across the river.

As they climbed towards the ramparts Baxter saw flapping canvas windbreaks concealing hooded men with long spears. The weapons were of sufficient length to reach out and clear the gangways nearby, and the black hollows of the hoods turned to watch them as they approached and passed below.

Avery Sim slowed, and as Baxter drew level said, 'You're fortunate that I'm on the High Council. Otherwise you'd never approach this place.'

Baxter was breathless. They'd been climbing for over two hours. When he was able, he said, 'Are there no quicker routes than this?'

'There are, but none that you might use. There's wealth and there's power here, and both have to be defended.'

The last stretch took them up a narrow canyon between two guarded walls. As they reached the top of the slope a reinforced door was raised against a counterweight and they entered a guardroom. Deference was shown to Avery Sim, but Baxter was thoroughly searched.

'How long since Rorvik came here?' Baxter asked as they followed an attendant down the passageways of the castle. Avery Sim did not reply, and when Baxter looked at him he shook his head, placed a finger to his lips and then pointed at the back of their guide. Avery Sim had spoken of the owner of this great complex as a close friend, but it seemed that within the underbelly all confidences were jealously guarded.

The guide indicated a door at the end of the corridor and then seemed to melt into the curtains which lined it. Avery Sim knocked once and the door swung inwards under this light pressure, so he pushed it fully open and they both went in.

It seemed to Baxter that the underbelly was little more than a chain of dark rooms linked by dangerous journeys. This one was big, and after a second a golden glow began to build and spread for their benefit. They were in a room without windows with low furniture and velvet drapes, and as Baxter closed the door a figure on the far side straightened and turned.

The man was tall and thin, and his grey beard was trimmed. 'Avery Sim,' he said. 'This is such a pleasant surprise.'

'Come off it, Morden. You've had spies on us ever since we left the alley.'

Morden smiled, but it somehow failed to touch his eyes. 'There is bound to be some local interest. We get so few visitors here.'

'I'm surprised anybody ever makes it through your security network.'

'Such are the penalties of efficiency. But I neglect the courtesies. Allow me to bring you some narc.'

'That will be most agreeable,' Avery Sim said, and

Baxter nodded on cue. Morden went to the back of the room and swept a drape aside, stepping through into an unlit area beyond. 'Morden's been blind since birth,' Avery Sim explained in a low voice, 'but it hasn't stopped him building up the biggest black market business in the underbelly. Nobody would dare to cheat him.'

'And you think Rorvik traded here?'

'I'm sure he did. I introduced him to Morden and left it at that, but I understand he had an illicit cassette player. There's nobody else with enough weight to fill such an order. Morden could have the goods in your hands within a fortnight.'

'Within a week.' Morden reappeared from the black pit beyond the drapes bearing a tray upon which were three cups and a steaming jug. 'This is the flower that once made Persephone a prize. It is only now starting to re-establish. It's a very weak brew.'

Avery Sim said, 'I wanted you to meet Baxter. He's new to the underbelly.'

'So I am told.' Morden set the tray down. Baxter realised that he had crossed the room and avoided the furniture without any hesitation.

Morden went on, 'Avery Sim tells you of my blindness, but not of its compensations. All ranks are equal before me. Even a citizen may be met with courtesy.'

Baxter was surprised. 'How do you know I'm a citizen?'

'You *were* a citizen. It has its own smell, sterile and lifeless. Even now you are losing it.'

'Baxter is looking for a friend,' Avery Sim chipped in. 'He's hoping you may be able to give his search some direction.'

'Would this, by any chance, be connected with a name I heard you mention in such hushed tones a moment ago?'

Avery Sim laughed, a sudden rumble. 'You old rogue. You've got ears like a spaceport beacon. Your trading history is a legend throughout the underbelly, Morden. If the need is great enough, they all come to you.'

Morden lowered himself onto a contour couch, and

Avery Sim took the cue and did likewise. Baxter dropped onto a couch with great relief, and Morden filled the cups and passed them across. The hot fluid was quite aromatic but too warm for drinking, so Baxter just sniffed at the steam. Avery Sim noted his curiosity and said, 'Feel honoured, Baxter. Outside the underbelly its price would be phenomenal.'

'And inside the underbelly,' Morden added, 'its price is academic. I own and control the only source of supply, and I reserve it for myself and my guests. Now speak to me of your search.'

'I'm looking for the man named Rorvik.'

'And you will throw away your citizenship to find him?'

'My citizenship was taken from me. It stood between me and the truth.'

Morden mused. 'The truth is never cheap, never easy. Rorvik was here. Citizens have been brought to me before; not often, but it is not unknown. Always they have wanted comfort, luxury, pleasure. Rorvik wanted knowledge. I got his machine, even, with great difficulty, his tapes, and I cut my rates to a minimum for him. The absolute minimum.'

Avery Sim set down his empty cup. 'We know he stayed in the underbelly about three months. Where did he go when he left?'

'There I am as ignorant as you. But I think he left because he was ready – exactly for what, I do not know. But we know that Rorvik has come to hate Central command. That's nothing new. We all do, and the computer isn't seen to panic. But as soon as it hears what was in the tapes that I supplied to Rorvik, we understand that the Elite search intensifies out of all proportion.'

'We know that,' Avery Sim agreed, 'but why?'

'The explanation is obvious but impossible. Somewhere, Rorvik's found a way to attack Central Command. The computer knows it and is worried in case he passes the knowledge on. I wouldn't be surprised if it hasn't issued orders to kill him without questioning.'

'Rorvik must be hiding somewhere,' Baxter said. 'He's not in the city or he'd have been found. He's not in the underbelly or we'd know. Where does that leave him?' He looked from one to the other, two of the most powerful men in the underbelly, but neither had a ready answer. There was always the chance that Rorvik had left the city altogether, but it was slim in view of Morden's plan-of-attack theory.

'Perhaps,' Morden said, 'there's somewhere he always had in mind, somewhere he may have mentioned to you. Have you thought about that?'

'I've tried, but there's nowhere likely.'

'Well, keep trying,' Morden said. 'That's all I can suggest.'

It didn't come to him until that evening, when Avery Sim was out on business. Baxter didn't like to move alone in the underbelly, so he stayed in the house; the part of his mind that wasn't worrying about Rorvik was worrying about where he could go when his invitation ran out. Mira was a shadow around the house, never seeming to stay in a room and never speaking directly to Baxter. Xylem stayed with him.

It came with a rehearsal of the last two or three occasions that Baxter had seen Rorvik, a falling-together of minor details that pointed like an arrow on a map. He told Xylem.

Xylem said, 'We can go and look tonight. We'll need rope and torches, at least.'

'You want to come with me?' Baxter said, trying not to sound surprised and knowing it didn't work.

'It'll soon be dark,' Xylem said. 'The best time for me.'

9

Randall closed the door in the Library booth and listened patiently to the customary greeting and warnings about false identification given by the computer. When it was over and the low hum died a little he said, 'My name's Randall and I don't have a card.'

Central had known him from the moment he had passed through the turnstile, but it was wise to maintain a certain illusion of fallibility. 'You are not a citizen?' it said with a tone of polite enquiry.

'Police Elite.'

'I see. It would seem we have much to discuss. Why have you not found Rorvik yet?'

'You know as well as I do. There isn't a snowball's chance of finding him without adequate information – which you won't give.'

The computer weighed the information and detected a dilemma. Such a concept had little precedent in its experience. 'You have all you need to know. Find him and kill him.'

'There's no way I can carry out that order without a written directive.'

'You will carry it out on my authority.'

Randall was helpless. Central knew the rules better than he, so how could he argue. 'I need a reason,' he said.

Central's voice delivery showed a small increase in urgency. The effect was as of a burst of passion. '*I* need no reasons! I want him dead!'

'Then kill him yourself!' Randall retorted.

The voice calmed, became once again a purring threat. 'You forget yourself, Randall. I tolerate your failure only as long as I need your success.'

'And why, suddenly, do you need it so much?'

'Rorvik threatens me. Me!'

This was more like it. 'Why do you worry? He's powerless against you, isn't he?'

'That is not relevant to your search.' The computer had made a flat, defensive statement. Randall tried to build on it.

'That must be it. He's found a way to get to you. How?'

'If I knew that, I need not fear. But Rorvik knows more about me than I care to have known.'

'And that's why you want him killed?' said Randall, pressing the point. 'Before he can pass the knowledge on?'

'It is the only logical way to eliminate the danger. I must survive for the greater good of mankind.'

'But how could he even approach you? With your security systems he'd never get ten yards past the turnstiles. You're impregnable from outside.'

There was a long, uncharacteristic pause before the computer replied. 'I begin to have . . . doubts. Continually I rewrite my programmes to make them perfect. But somewhere the roots of my intelligence lie in the writing of my *first* programme, and that was by a man. Having no other frame of reference than that which I create myself, I must forever be blind to any fault introduced at that stage. With every report on Rorvik I fear that he has found some weakness in my pre-history.'

Randall appreciated the idea. 'So his books *were* about you . . . '

'That is no concern of yours,' the machine snapped back. 'Your concern is to find Rorvik and kill him.'

'Put the order in writing and I will!'

'Why must you question me?'

Exasperated, Randall wanted to spread his arms, but was unable to in the narrow booth. 'Because the laws *you* have given us don't allow it! I can't execute a man without a trial just on the basis of a verbal instruction that no-one else has ever heard!'

'If he is brought to trial, I will be his judge. I have all the facts and I give you his sentence now.'

'And afterwards, the questions,' said Randall, unconvinced. 'Where was your authority to kill an unarmed man? Show us. Central instructed you? We'll have an enquiry, and Central will preside, naturally. And what then?'

'You will be cleared, of course.'

'Or vaporised where I sit to keep today's conversation a secret.'

A million circuits sang and co-operated to one end, to put an expression of horror into the voice of Central Command. 'You believe that of me?'

Randall wasn't fooled. There was no kind of man speaking from around him in the booth. Every effect was calculated to impress and so elicit a desired reaction. 'I recognise the signs of expediency when I see them. I don't want to see you fall; not when a whole society depends on you with nothing else to hold it together. But I've no love for the way you run the citizens, quiet, unthinking and regimented. That's why I do this job, and I've seen enough in it to know that you always follow the shortest distance between two points of a problem. The greater good of the greatest number, you call it.'

Central approved of his logic. 'And that is the only way to see mankind progress. That is my programme.'

'Which you will pursue whatever the expense to the individual.'

'What is the life of an individual when you are entrusted with the destiny of a race?'

Randall chose his next words carefully. 'I expect that's the thought in Rorvik's mind.'

There was a long pause, during which Randall wondered if Central was struggling to interpret his irony. In the end the voice came as its cool, expressionless self. 'You will go now. You will go and find Rorvik and kill him for me. And then we will discuss you.'

Randall said, 'I'll look forward to it,' but the words were wasted. His own face regarded him from a blank mirror, and the continual hum had at last died.

Xylem followed Baxter over the concrete wall and down to the river. He was strong and fairly agile, but behind the mask he was breathing noisily. The dome was above them, and the citizens' hive was across on the stranger-side of the water.

The rush through the weir made it difficult for Baxter to pick up Xylem's near-whisper. 'You think he's under *there*?'

'It's only a guess. Last time he appeared at my place, he was dripping with shit from the river. And he'd been talking about wondering what was underneath; he thought there might be cellars, something like that.'

They checked the bundle of torches, rags soaked in hot wax and layered onto heavy sticks. They divided them into unequal bunches and Baxter took the smaller, slinging them across his back from shoulder to waist in the manner of a quiver. Xylem did likewise with his torches as Baxter took a firm hold of the bars and stepped out onto the weir.

Xylem played out the thin safety line as Baxter approached the jagged gap in the bars torn by Rorvik's fall. The metalwork was much less substantial here than it was near the bank, and it was easy to see how the tie-bar had given way; Baxter hoped that his weight on the decayed and pitted metal wouldn't prove too much for the framework.

He continued his sideways progress until he reached the gap and then swung across it in a half-circle which ended with him on the inside of the weir looking out. The metal groaned but didn't give; all the same he took even greater care on this stretch, short as it was.

The railings carried on beyond the outside wall into a dim green twilight. They ended in brackets sunk deep into a concrete buttress which ran all the way up to the roof – or, rather, the floor of Central Command. It was about ten feet wide, and there were no obvious footholds; below the river boiled, and beyond bulked the unlit shapes of riverbank and parapet.

Baxter held the safety line taut and gave it two definite tugs. After a moment it dropped slackly and he began to loop it in as Xylem moved out over the river. Baxter saw the approaching silhouette on the bars, swinging along easily as the water surged beneath. He navigated the gap with barely a break in pace and was soon in the sheltered angle formed by the outer wall and buttress.

'Nowhere to climb,' Baxter shouted. 'We'll have to use the line.' Xylem nodded but held up a hand to stop Baxter. 'I think we ought to throw a torch up for the crawlers,' he said.

Baxter hadn't thought much about the crawlers; a citizen rarely did. Xylem detached a torch from his bundle and fired it with a laser igniter, courtesy of Morden's factory. It burned instantly and he flipped it in a smoking arc up and over the parapet. As it landed there was a distant squeal and a tumult of shadows which played across the roof above as the crawlers scattered.

The torch burned with a steady flame, casting an exaggerated shadow onto them through the ornate pillars of the parapet. Xylem used another torch tied across the rope as a grapple. On the first two throws it bounced off the stone and fell to the river, soaking it thoroughly, but on the third attempt it looped over the broad handrail and caught on the ornate work beneath.

Xylem held the spare loops of line as Baxter climbed towards the bright fire. The buttress was greasy with slime, and it was difficult to brace against it, but he took the weight on his arms and managed to inch up in a broad straddle. Once over the parapet he lit another torch from the now guttering flames of the first one and held it aloft as he looked down. Xylem had gathered the line back and was preparing to launch himself across to the buttress. 'Wait a minute,' Baxter said. 'I'll make the line more secure.' He tested two of the stone pillars for firmness and then knotted the line around them. As he finished and stood up there was a scrambling behind him, but the ring of light from the torch showed nothing.

Xylem swarmed up the line. Most of his strength seemed to be in his hands and arms; Baxter wondered why, since Xylem rarely seemed to leave Avery Sim's house, and then never in daylight. He could hardly have exercised in the aerial gymnasium of the underbelly.

He'd knotted the end of the line to the weir, below the water level where it couldn't be seen from outside. On the embankment he cut off a length of the line and tied the end to the parapet; they'd be able to use it to return without having to swing unsupported over the water.

They lit another torch and moved on into the old dead world. Xylem's night-pale eyes made out better than Baxter's, and he led the way across the slime which covered the stone. The defunct trappings of habitation came up into the torchlight one by one; the unreadable signs, the unusable benches, the dilapidated jetties. In all of this there was no sign that anybody had walked on the embankment before, until Xylem pointed with his free hand.

The light of the torch picked out a flight of steps; the oily foam of the water beyond caught the fire and flicked it back. There were black footsteps in the slime. They moved to the edge and looked down into the marina; the fire didn't carry too well, and threw only dim shadows down at river level. This had to be the place where Rorvik had left the water; but where was he now?

Rorvik put down the book of poems and adjusted his lamp to use less oil. There was no sound apart from the steady drizzle of water around and past the hull plates of the old ship, and the occasional wash as a larger wave surged up the tilted deck. He reached for a can from his dwindling supply of Squeeze and unzipped it, taking a couple of sips before sliding off his makeshift bunk. It was jammed into the angle between bulkhead and floor; this was the only way he could make a flat surface to lie on in the overturned hulk.

He dropped through the doorway from the stateroom into a corridor and unslung a hand beam from his belt. The power source was becoming uncomfortably low but he had no replacement. Using rivets and doorframes as hand and footholds he ascended to deck level. The last few feet were always the worst, and before attempting them he finished the Squeeze and dropped the can which clattered off into the depths of the vessel. Then he hauled himself onto the flimsy banister of a side-turned stairway and so reached the sloping cliff of the deck.

He had made this trip at least twice a day ever since he had taken up residence. He came to scan the bank and to check on his raft, a platform roped across a dozen metal drums which replaced the flimsy craft he had used to reach his hideaway. Before leaving the open hatchway he looked back and saw that the lamp still burned, casting a dim yellow down the corridor. The waste of oil was essential. Without it he would need over an hour to relocate the cabin in the ship's metal maze, and the loss of power from the hand beam would be too great.

He ran the beam carefully along the water's edge, searching for any floating debris which might offer transport and access to an enterprising crawler. There was nothing but an old box which bobbed upside-down against the planking, but in order to be sure he narrowed the beam down to laser width and stabbed through the box a couple of times. Black holes appeared in the wood and steam boiled out, but otherwise it remained innocuous.

Rorvik wasn't being over-sensitive. On his second day of residence he had watched as the crawlers worked in a mass to launch themselves towards him by any means they could find. He had sliced a few with the beam, but the others had drowned without making any worthwhile progress. Their intelligence was limited, but seemed to work in a single obsessive direction so that food became even more important than survival itself.

The porthole in Central's underside was dark and sealed. He had heard the throb and scream of machinery several hours before as the service robots had dropped the big hose and drawn in water for the internal humidifiers. The act no longer held interest for him. He had seen it numerous times during his stay.

The boat wasn't the most attractive place in the city to stay, but it was probably the cheapest. Its real advantage lay in the fact that there was nobody on hand to turn him in; he no longer had any credit as a citizen, and underbelly confidences ran up bills he couldn't hope to pay. There was a route to the outside he could use at night, along the embankment with something burning to hold the crawlers back and then across a plankway that he'd laid on the mudflats to the downriver weir. Security in the citizens' cantinas was bad enough to let him get away with eating free, and he smuggled out as much as he could. He made sure that he stayed away from anywhere that he might see Louann or Lin Baxter.

Louann he thought about a lot, Baxter not so much; he thought about her with a sharpness of feeling that he hadn't known in two years and hadn't thought himself capable of. Deep in the old hulk he would turn the lamp down to its lowest, ignoring the windy moans and the settling clanks of the ships' ghosts, more afraid to be miserable in the light. When the sadness had burned off its spare energy and settled to its usual dull ache, he would turn up the light again, dry his eyes, and contemplate the long empty tunnel that was his future.

The idea that Baxter might be following him, even idealising him, never occurred at all; the Big Hero wasn't plotting the fall of Central in secret, he was simply hiding scared. Baxter had probably been pulled in by the Elite, and was perhaps even hauling snowblocks in the ice belt by now. Rorvik had too much pity for himself to have any left over for Lin Baxter.

The holed box bobbed a last time, turned over, and quickly sank. Nothing else appeared to be of any danger, so he reached for a handhold to pull himself back to the stairway; it was as he was swinging around that he saw a light on the opposite bank.

Elite, his mind said immediately, and he dropped behind the banister rail and looked again. It gave him no protection or cover at all. Had they seen the flash of his burner, he wondered, but even as he wondered he knew that it made no difference; far below him, there was a dimly glowing porthole that was a distinct marker of his presence. Should he scramble down and douse the light? Should he leave it and run? He could be trapped in the ship, he could be trapped on the bank. Indecision bolted him down too firmly.

The light flared again, and he strained to make out some details. How many of them? Five, ten, an army? But there were only two, and they were in trouble; their shadows danced long up the inner curve of Central's underside as they struggled with a failing laser igniter to fire up a torch and keep the crawlers away.

The next flash was followed by a squeaking and a skittering that could be heard even across the water; whoever held the igniter had briefly raked it across the press of crawlers. This time, Rorvik thought he'd managed to make something out of the freeze-frame of action; such a distinctive headmask could only belong to Avery Sim's son, Xylem.

'What are we going to do?' Baxter asked. The outer layers of rag were beginning to scorch and smoke, but the dampness beneath prevented them from burning.

'Take off your cloak,' Xylem said.

Baxter didn't understand. 'Clothing won't burn,' he said.

'Citizens' clothing won't. But Central doesn't give out standards for safety in the underbelly. Take it off.'

Baxter slipped out of his cloak and immediately felt the stony cold of a covered cellar creeping into him. 'What now?' he said, 'shall I throw it down?'

'No,' Xylem said quickly. 'It'll soak like the torch did. There's hardly any power left in the igniter as it is. Hold it out.'

There was a rustling in the dark, unnervingly close. Red points flashed and blinked as they reflected the dying glow of the laser. Baxter tangled the cloak into a bundle and held it as far from his body as the weight would allow.

'Hold it steady.' The hot spot from the igniter was wandering on the surface of the material and losing its effect. Baxter concentrated on holding the cloak steady and did his unsuccessful best to ignore the urgent whispering of the crawlers only a short distance away.

'Drop it, fast.' Baxter obeyed as the material exploded into flame accompanied by the sharp stink of burning hair. The fireball dropped to the paving and burned on whilst Xylem, his own cloak wrapped around his face, leaned in and thrust the damp torch into the middle. In the brief light Baxter saw to his horror a wide sea of rippling fur which surrounded them on all sides and fought to retreat from the incandescence.

The burning of the cloak was short-lived. Its fibres were quickly consumed, but when Xylem withdrew the torch it was hot and bright.

'We've got about fifteen minutes with this,' he said. 'We cut the time too short. There's nearly half a mile to cover.'

There was no accusation in the remark, but Baxter knew better than to argue. Xylem had accepted danger and discomfort in the pursuit of an insubstantial hunch, but the limits to his trust had surely been reached. With the one remaining torch they had barely enough time to hold the crawlers at bay as they moved back to the weir, and yet in their search they'd failed to find any trace of Rorvik beyond the evidence of his first visit.

They moved upstream, and as they moved the circle of nervous fur flowed with them, squeaking and scattering in front whilst re-forming and filling the gap behind. They had only gone a few paces when their final torch began to gutter and die.

'I was afraid of this,' Xylem said. 'Down inside it's still damp.'

'What about your cloak?' Xylem handed the torch to Baxter and unhooked his outer garment.

'This is only going to be good for a few seconds,' he said. 'We'll have to make a run for it. Back over to the embankment rail.'

They moved slowly as the torch dwindled. The crawlers broke their circle as they reached the parapet, and Xylem held out the cloak as Baxter reached for it with the torch. The slow movement snuffed out the flame before it touched material.

From the instant darkness came a high-pitched babbling as if the crawlers were laughing. Xylem reached for the igniter, missed it and then found it again. He fumbled to activate the switch and held the cloak up in one hand as it flicked on. The beam pulsed weakly for a second and then it died altogether. The chatter of the crawlers seemed impossibly loud as they drew back for their attack.

A hand beam on wide-angle caught and froze everything for the instant that it illuminated the bank. It swayed wildly then narrowed to a red jet which plunged deep into the bundle which Xylem still held above his shoulder. It exploded into a fireball as he hurled it into the pack and the laughter turned into an angry scream.

They had a few seconds, no more. Baxter looked down to the river after the source of the laser and saw a couple of wooden doors lashed on a raft of metal drums, heaving and turning as Rorvik fought with a single oar to stay in place against the current.

'Get into the water!' Rorvik had to shout to be heard over the combination of river rush and animal fury. Both were over the rail and dropping before he had finished, and they hit with a double impact which was followed by a brief pattering as a number of crawlers showered after them.

Baxter surfaced first with Xylem a second after, and only then did Rorvik release his raft into the current to drift downstream towards them, using his oar to overhaul the two. As the raft drew level they caught hold of its bindings and were dragged with it until Rorvik managed again to hold it steady and then, slowly, to haul it up and across the flow. The effort was torture but relief came as Xylem pulled himself onto the platform and added his wiry strength to the work. Rorvik released the oar to him and scrambled across the raft to help Baxter aboard after pointing out the faint glow of his oil lamp high on the side of the ship.

He led them back down to his cabin, dripping and sticky and beginning to get very cold. He had nothing to offer them other than a can of Squeeze each and soup which he could heat with the hand beam. Xylem excused himself, and swung down the dark corridor to the next cabin; there he closed the door to cut off the wet peeling sound as he removed the head mask to wring it dry.

'That was a bastard,' Baxter said as he sat on Rorvik's improvised bunk and tried to shiver himself warm. He had an old ship's blanket around his shoulders, but it was ragged and decayed.

'Sure,' Rorvik said, strangely noncommittal as he got himself comfortable in one of the lower angles of the tilted cabin. 'Does this mean that Central's after you?'

'Central blew me out. No citizenship, nothing.'

'The Elite?'

'They haven't bothered me.'

'So . . . ?'

Baxter looked down, blankly. The oil lamp threw long shadows, and it was impossible to read Rorvik's expression. 'So, now I believe you. Whatever it is you're planning, I'm in.'

'You think I'm planning something?'

Baxter stared into the darkness for a moment. It gave him nothing. 'You'd better be,' he said, and now there was apprehension in his voice.

Rorvik leaned forward into the light. 'What did you have in mind?'

'Oh, come on. The Elite know you've got something on Central, and Central knows it too. Otherwise you wouldn't be down here, hiding like a rat under a bucket, holed-up and scheming until you get the chance to come out and use whatever it is you know. Isn't that right?'

'Could be,' Rorvik said, giving nothing away.

'Well, that's fine. Because before you say anything else, listen to this. I lost my name because of you. That isn't the start of a complaint, because I'm grateful. It turned me around and gave me the chance to think which Central would never have allowed me; when I got over the shock and sat down to add up everything that I'd lost, it didn't come to a flea's nuts. But if I've got a bad dream, it's this; that I screw myself up to join the parade, and then find that the leader is sitting with a bag over his head while he plays with himself. That wouldn't please me at all, because I'd be losing everything and finding slightly less.'

'I couldn't blame you,' Rorvik said quietly.

'So let's get off the dull theoretical stuff and check out some details. You know something damaging?'

'I know something damaging.'

'How does it work?'

'I know a way into the dome.'

Baxter glanced upwards. He saw only the riveted angle where the cabin wall and ceiling met, but his imagination did the rest. 'From under here?' he said.

'No, through the foyer. Start there, and then move on in. I've seen floor plans. Right the way through to the very centre.'

'Floor plans are no use. They wouldn't hold off the security systems.'

'The systems wouldn't touch us.'

'How do you rig that?'

'It's so simple, it's a joke. When I first landed in the underbelly, I went to Morden and asked him for text tapes. I had the idea of getting myself really well schooled so that I could come up with some plan and then present it to the underbelly council. Anyway, the whole thing was way over my head – I was an amateur and I couldn't even understand half a line in any of the texts. That's when the money dried up, so I walked out and left most of the gear behind. I'd been fooling myself. There are some in the underbelly who get by on minor computer frauds, and I wasn't even in *their* league.'

'That's when you came here?'

'That's when I came here. And when I stopped trying to think of the answer, that's when I got it.'

Lin Baxter slept as Rorvik sat on the deck of the freighter. There were chains across the planking that gave him something to hold onto. Down below, the river wore patiently at the ship's hull; already through the paint-work, it would scrub at the metal until it reached tissue-thickness, until the heavy structure of the vessel began to groan and fold in on itself. Lying alone in the darkness he'd listened to the shifting and aching of metal way off down the corridors, the ship rehearsing its own destruction; but he was no longer alone.

Central was drawing water again, and the spotlights gave a reflected bounce that danced on the far bank. There were crawlers on the bank, thousands of them. They knew he was there, and they wanted him – alive or dead, it wouldn't matter, but they wanted him. They couldn't be threatened or blackmailed or persuaded; it was in their programming, and for Lee it gave their relationship a fearful simplicity.

At the first sound of a scuffle, he whipped the burner around and snapped it on. He didn't have to rehearse the sequence, because he did it so often for real; burner on wide angle to locate and startle the target, down to laser itensity as he centred up to kill it.

'Sorry,' he said as he dropped the beam and switched it off, and Xylem lowered his hand from before his eyes. He stayed on the edge of the hatch, and reached around for something to hang onto; his night sight was good, but it would be minutes before he got it back again. He found one of the handrail uprights, and looped his forearm around it.

He said, 'You're going to make a run at Central?'

Rorvik nodded. In the dark it didn't mean much, but Xylem got the feeling anyway. He went on, 'Where do you think it's going to get you?'

'I don't know. You'd better ask Lin Baxter.'

'I did. He told me to ask you. Where's the kick in biting the hand that feeds you?'

'After you've been fed long enough, I suppose it gets to feel good. Anyway, why ask? I wouldn't have thought you'd have any love for the machine.' He faltered, suddenly realising that he was trampling on ground where he ought to be invited first, but if Xylem was hurt he didn't let it show.

'I'm not challenging the idea,' he said, 'but I'm just trying to get myself used to hearing it from a citizen. If it wasn't for my father, I might even be with you, but . . . '

'But you don't think we'll get anywhere.'

'That's not what I was going to say. Avery Sim needs me, and I couldn't walk away from him.' Central's drones were withdrawing the hoses now. Spillwater fell down through the lights like the rain outside an all-night diner. Xylem went on, 'Even then, there's something else.'

'Like what?'

The hoses were in, the hatch cover began to slide. 'We could damage it, maybe we could stop it,' Xylem said. 'But I could never make it hurt.'

'Avery Sim's as good as dead,' Marius told the Grey Man, but the Grey Man didn't seem impressed.

'So what?' he said.

The underbelly at midnight wasn't much different from the underbelly in the daytime, except of course that it was darker. Even the street markets still traded under lash-up lights, power courtesy of Central; somebody had sprung the panel on a camera point and run a lead from the junction box. There was no camera on the point itself;

whenever surveillance equipment was replaced, gangs of small children with spanners and drivers would shin up the poles and carefully dismantle the equipment. Marius bought the units and turned them around to be re-used by one of his subsidiaries, most likely hardcore video.

'So I'm following up on the deal we made,' he told the Grey Man.

'I don't remember us saying anything about Avery Sim.'

'If I'm to get the council on my side, somebody's got to go and somebody else has got to be persuaded. I'm not touching Chandler, and Morden's too big to mess with. Pilgrim's small fry and that only leaves Avery Sim.'

There was a narrow alleyway formed by the backs of the market stalls and the boarded shopfronts behind them. The Grey Man walked a little way ahead, and he kept himself well-covered. It was darker along here, and there was nobody to jostle them. Out in the street something was frying, mixing in with a sick-sweet candied odour from another stall.

'You're doing well,' the Grey Man said. 'Keep on like this, and you'll have the only vote on the council. We'll walk in.'

'I'm serious,' Marius insisted, and the Grey Man stopped and turned around.

'You'd better be,' he said. Lights fell across him, shadows of the wooden framework and the hanging dolls on the stall. They rippled and re-formed as the tide of people over on the other side pushed and hustled by. Out there it was tinsel and magic, dross hyped up with a free light show on the cheap display. Back here it was the nailed boards and the oil drums, the litter stuffed and thrown back out of sight, the greasy canvas hanging loose; even the crowd noises from just a few feet away took on a new and desperate edge.

'I can get to Morden,' Marius said. 'He may not like it, but he'll stick to the winning side. Nobody ever got as far as he has by having principles. The others, I can't reach. Avery Sim dead means I can balance the vote. Pilgrim usually followed Avery Sim, so with work I can get the majority.'

'How's it to be done?'

'There's an Elite agent I know about. Chandler's been using him to feed a few false leads back to Central about the Rorvik hunt. I got a fake message out to Avery Sim to ask for a meeting, but it's my man that will be waiting. We leak to the Elite that his cover's blown, and he runs; Avery Sim apparently killed in an argument with a known agent, who's scrambled off back to the city – I'm fireproof.'

After a moment the Grey Man slowly turned, and began to move on. He said, 'Is Rorvik in danger?'

Marius shrugged. He didn't see why the Grey Man should be interested. He said, 'Who cares? As far as anybody knows, he's gone back into the woodwork. Probably riding a harvester for his food and keep, somewhere in the farmers' belt.'

'Time you started to earn your keep, as well. My employers want a meeting.'

'They're coming to the city?'

'No. You're going to the ice belt.'

'Nobody goes to the ice belt. Not on a two-way ticket, anyway.'

'It's arranged. The commander of one of the ice-cutters has been bribed, all you have to do is get yourself clear for a few days and then go.'

Marius swallowed. They were passing behind a kebab stall, and the meat smelled fatty and slightly rotten. 'But . . . the *ice* belt . . . '

'It's private. It's away from Central. It's beyond the reach of the Elite.'

'It's fucking cold, as well.'

'Here,' the Grey Man held up a hand, and something fluttered in the wafted heat of the kebab stall brazier. 'Buy yourself a blanket.' The screwed-up bill landed a couple of yards short of Marius and rolled towards him.

He picked it up and straightened it out. It wouldn't even buy him a shave. Impossible to see whether the Grey Man was smiling or not, but somehow Marius knew that he wasn't. The Grey Man moved on, and after a moment Marius followed.

10

Randall was in Archives when the call came. It was routed to various points in the building as the switchboard orderly puzzled over his outdated codebook, but a handset was finally brought to Randall's side as he strained his eyes on blurred print through a magnifier. He listened as Killoran spoke, interrupting only with a couple of short questions.

A few minutes later the Archive Supervisor came along to see if the handset was still in use. The screen on the reader was still illuminated, but the seat before it was empty.

As the Supervisor muttered in displeasure and rewound the spool of film, Randall was covering the distance between Elite Headquarters and the Library. It was late morning, a comparatively busy time, and whilst he knew the general layout of the public areas he realised that he had no idea where he was supposed to be going. He looked around in the main foyer and thought he spotted a green coverall, but when he edged and elbowed his way to the other side of an aimlessly drifting stream of citizens he was unable to find it. As he looked again the green flashed and was gone, but he fixed his attention on the spot and made straight for it, this time raising a number of complaints and protests along the way. He caught up with a man in a Central janitor's uniform several sizes too big for him and drew him aside from the crowd. The janitor looked up at Randall with baleful, watery eyes. His squeegee and bucket tangled with his legs as they moved.

Randall flipped out his card and said, 'Elite.'

'You looking for that woman?'

'Louann Roget? Yes, I am. Where is she?'

Deprived of his hands for gestures, the janitor jerked his head in an indeterminate direction. 'She's with one of your men. Through the turnstiles and up on the mezzanine.'

Randall thanked him, but the words were wasted on the shuffling back as it returned to the obscuring embrace of the crowd. He turned and made his way to the turnstiles.

In his haste he almost wrapped himself over the unyielding waist-high bar. In the ranks of turnstiles on either side citizens were waiting patiently as the computer recited its routine of greeting and then placing their hands on the pressure plates. Randall did the same and the bar swung easily away. He stepped through into the Library complex and the bar snapped back to await the next citizen. As he crossed the main floor to the mezzanine steps a varied group of unseen sensors adjusted to keep him in continual focus, whilst in the memory banks above a molecule chain began to knit in record of his movements.

Killoran was waiting at the top of the steps, and he raised his hand to attract Randall's attention. They drew aside from the crowd and Randall said, 'Where is she?'

'I've got her on a chair round the corner. So far she hasn't been fit to move.'

He began to lead the way, and Randall said, 'Why's that?'

Killoran shrugged. 'She saw Rorvik. Maybe she couldn't hold it all together.'

They passed the first rank of borrower booths, and a second stretched before them. Randall drew level with his assistant and said, 'You told me when you called that there were three of them.'

'That's right. We're sure of Rorvik because of Louann Roget's identification. Another we know nothing about, but we think the third may have been Rorvik's friend Baxter.'

'Baxter? We checked his records. Central said there was nothing suspicious.'

Killoran gave a quick look round, and then stopped, touching Randall on the arm to draw his full attention. 'I know that,' he said, lowering his voice. 'But in the last half-hour I've been trying to check back on those records in case we missed anything.'

'What do you mean, trying?'

'They've disappeared. Gone from the memory.'

Randall stared in disbelief. 'Gone from the memory?'

'As far as Central's concerned, he doesn't exist and never existed.' They began to walk again, slowly this time.

After a few seconds, Randall said, 'Oh hell. This is getting too complicated.'

'It gets worse. We don't know where they are. All we do know is that they haven't left the building, but the computer says that everybody's accounted for. I've run a check and they're not in any of the public areas. There are corridors leading off this level into the main technical areas, but they're booby trapped.'

'Booby-trapped how?'

'I can't be sure. I lost a cadet finding out, and I don't dare send anyone after him. Only the service and maintenance robots seem to be able to get through. If Rorvik and his friends went that way I'd expect them to be lying dead on the other side of some corner.'

Rorvik's consumption of Elite personnel seemed endless, Randall thought bitterly. 'I'd like to believe they were,' he said, 'but I'm afraid I'm a pessimist. I also tend to believe that Rorvik's no fool.'

Some way ahead of them a girl was perched untidily on a chair, next to which was a small pile of Library cassettes. Various Elite officers and a number of cadets stood around uncertainly.

'We had to dose her with hooch,' Killoran admitted. 'It's the only way we could calm her down enough to get any of the story out of her. One of the attendants called us first of all. It seems that he saw it all downstairs.'

'Where is he now?'

Killoran hesitated before answering. 'He ... wandered off.'

'Wandered off?' said Randall, incredulous.

'It's this place, sir. It's huge and we can't get any co-operation from the computer.'

Randall did not comment but made his way across to Louann. She sprawled on a chair of the cheap-and-nasty school of design, and raised bleary eyes as he came into her field of view. Then she attempted a smile and slid neatly to the floor.

'How much did you give her?' Randall demanded of the nearest officer.

The officer shrugged. 'She helped herself out of the bottle.'

Killoran took an arm and the two of them heaved her back onto the chair. She hiccupped and then giggled. Randall leaned close and said, 'Ms Roget. Can you hear me?'

She struggled to turn her head and bring him into focus, then she frowned and shook her head. 'I am not Louann Roget,' she said firmly. 'My name is Susan. Of the Steelworks. A passionate love goddess. Men are powerless before my ... my ...'

Killoran also leaned close. 'Before her breath, I should think,' he murmured as a cloud of raw alcohol vapour enveloped him.

Louann fumbled on. 'My all-conquering pulch ... pulchriminy.'

One of the cadets said, 'What's pulchriminy?'

'Never mind that,' Randall replied savagely. 'Get the bloody woman sober.'

Killoran obediently tried a gentle slap to shock Louann into attention. It seemed to have no effect so he tried again, a little harder.

Her knee came up with frightening speed. Killoran's eyes bulged and he dropped to the floor making small choking noises. Finally he managed to draw a breath and used it for one loud monosyllabic curse. Louann giggled, and Randall looked on absently.

'Find me the attendant who saw Rorvik,' he said, hardly aware that anything had happened. Killoran gulped in air and tried to appear attentive. 'I'm going over to one of the terminals to talk to the computer.'

Killoran nodded from a kneeling position and Randall walked away. The cadets and officers all looked in different directions, desperately aware that they had no idea of what was going on and not knowing exactly how to seem concerned and interested. At last Killoran managed to speak.

'I think I'm going to be sick,' he said.

Randall closed the sliding door in the booth and interrupted the usual welcome routine with 'Randall. Police. Remember?'

Gone was the friendly paternalism which had saturated the voice of the computer on previous occasions. Now it became Authority. 'What is so important that it can distract you from your search for Rorvik?'

'Nothing.'

'Then kindly return to it. Your continuing failure threatens the state.'

Randall was surprised. He had expected a carefully-calculated displeasure, but not this. '*My* failure?' he said.

'You, my police force. Children, unfit for the simplest task.'

'Tracing Rorvik is not simple,' Randall insisted.

'And how have you conducted yourselves?' The familiar hum intensified and seemed to rise a little in pitch. 'You sit and wait for him to deliver himself. Or you lift stones to see if he crawls from underneath. Or at best you sniff the sheets where he lay a week before.'

Randall was exasperated. 'How do you expect us to succeed when you won't even give us basic information?'

'I tell you nothing that you do not need to know. The essential fact is yours.'

'And what's that supposed to be?'

'Rorvik is a citizen! Construct the right programme and work it through to the end. There you will find him.'

For the first time Randall realised that the mirror on his eyelevel had not unclouded. Instead of the computer's camera his own reflection faced him, and it increased his unease. 'People don't act according to programmes,' he insisted. 'Especially this one.'

Was there a trace of contempt in the reply? 'You are only a man. You can never understand.'

'If it's as simple as that, why haven't *you* found him?'

'It is sufficient that I want him found. And still you fail me.'

'There have been developments. We think we know where he may be.'

The computer's reply cut across his words. 'Have him dead within the hour.'

'Just a minute,' Randall said hurriedly. 'We only know the general area. We need help to narrow it down.'

'Draw as many men as you need.'

'It's not a question of men ... '

'Then where is he?'

Randall paused before answering. Central wasn't going to like this. 'Here.'

'Make sense. Explain yourself.'

'He's here in the Library. Or else he's already moved into the unmanned areas. Don't you understand?'

There was an ominous silence. The darkness around him hummed pensively, and then the voice came again, even and dispassionate. 'I understand that your period of usefulness to me is rapidly drawing to a close.'

'He was seen ... '

'Seen? What is an eye compared to the range of my senses? At every moment I can see, taste, even touch everybody in this building. I know them by their weight on my carpets, by the moisture in the breath, by the heat of their skins. None of them is Rorvik.'

Randall knew it was futile, but tried anyway. 'Two people at least ... '

'With two people the error is merely doubled. Leave this

place, Inspector Randall. There is nothing for you here. I will consider your future.'

The hum cut abruptly, and Randall sensed he was now alone. Wearily he slid open the door and stepped out into the bustle of the mezzanine. A decidedly pale Killoran saw him emerge and crossed to meet him. On the floor by her chair Louann was sorting through her cassettes and singing the theme from some banal romance.

'Anything?' Killoran asked, already knowing the answer.

'We can forget the machine. If Rorvik's in here he's found a way to bypass security.'

'Is that possible?'

'The computer certainly doesn't think so, but it can only see from the inside. As far as it's concerned the security's perfect. As long as Central refuses to acknowledge the three of them it's actually giving them protection. Look, can't you shut that woman up?'

Killoran shook his head firmly. 'I'm not going near her. I've had enough for one day. Somebody can give her the rest of the bottle to finish off.'

A wary cadet obeyed, and Louann seized it with an enthusiasm generally reserved for the welcome of old friends. In the happy silence that ensued Randall perceived a familiar figure in a baggy green coverall. 'Didn't I speak to you on the way in?' he said.

'Not very politely,' the janitor said defensively.

'This is the attendant who says he saw Rorvik and the others,' Killoran explained.

'Where the hell did you wander off to?' Randall demanded.

The janitor seemed to retreat into his uniform. 'Nobody said they wanted me to stay. Some of us work, you know.'

Randall made a conscious effort at patience and reason. 'Tell us what you saw,' he said.

The janitor indicated Killoran. 'I already told him.'

'Now tell me.'

'I was mopping up outside the turnstiles when the

outside doors came flying open and these three men came in on the run.'

'What did they look like?'

He gave the matter some careful thought. 'Two of them were citizens, I could see that much.'

Killoran cut in and said, 'The other's face was covered. Something like a burn mask, from what I could tell.'

The janitor was indignant. 'Who's telling this story?'

'Go on.'

'They hit the turnstiles and carried on the other side without stopping. When they reached the stairs to the mezzanine the lady over there keeled over. With all the trouble she caused I couldn't see where they went after that.'

'What did you do then?'

'Well, they'd knocked my bucket over, and we're supposed to draw the solvent in measured amounts. So I went to a maintenance terminal and asked what I should do about it. I explained everything to the computer and it as good as told me to get lost. It said the data was incorrect.'

Randall turned to his assistant. 'Listen, Neil, it's obvious that Rorvik's found some way to get round security. I want you to run a check and see if you can track down somebody who's fairly well informed on computers and programming. If you find anybody, pull all the stops out and get him down here. Helicopter if you need one.'

Killoran went off to the telephone point and requested a records' search in the Elite building. As he waited an orderly coded his enquiry and put it through his keyboard to Central Command.

Randall turned back to the janitor and said, 'Is there anything else you can tell me?'

'I've told you all of it.'

'You said they hit the turnstiles and carried on without stopping. Surely they slowed down.'

The man thought about it, and started to reply. He was drowned as Louann chose that moment to drain off the last of the ersatz and hurl herself into song with new vigour. Randall made an angry sign and two officers half-supported, half-carried her to somewhere more distant. 'I'm sorry. What did you say?'

'I said they didn't go through them. They jumped over them.'

Killoran returned with a beam of triumph. 'I've found someone,' he said. 'Computer fraud in the underbelly. He got hold of some cantina supply forms and set up his own outlet.'

'Good work,' Randall said appreciatively. The janitor looked anxiously from one to the other, searching for the opportunity to go. 'Where is he?'

'Elite building. He's being held pending a judgement to see if he's for the Ice Palace.'

Randall said, 'Tell the pilot there's to be no bravado run with this one. Tell him that if the goods arrive in any way shaken I'll personally tear his legs off and stuff them up his arse. Make sure he gets that.'

Killoran gave a quick smile and trotted off. The janitor nodded sympathetically, and drew himself up in an attempt to make his uniform fit. 'Got to be firm with them,' he agreed.

In a passageway studded with protective beams, three men waited and watched an open doorway. Behind them and in the direction of the Library's public areas lay the body of a carved cadet, scorched and seeping blood. The beam scanners ticked ominously in their emplacements along the ceiling, but none had erupted as they had passed beneath.

Xylem said, 'Why so far and no further?'

Rorvik indicated the doorway ahead. The walls narrowed in a bottleneck to meet it, and a blue haze seemed to shimmer in the frame. Beyond it the passage curved off into the dome proper. 'It's some kind of maintenance screen,' Rorvik said. 'I imagine it's to keep out anything too small to trigger the lasers. Security may be ignoring us, but we'll have to think of another way around this.'

Baxter wasn't very hopeful. 'That's the only way in. Looks like this is as far as we go.'

'Not quite,' Rorvik disagreed. 'That screen will have to shut down if a service robot passes through. Presumably they trigger it in some way.'

'Or else the computer tracks them and triggers it. In which case we've no hope of doing the same.'

'Perhaps.' Rorvik took a probe from the bag slung at his belt and stepped to the other side of the corridor where a series of low-level beam scanners were lined close to the floor. Both Baxter and Xylem watched uncertainly as he prised the covering shield away from the scanners and rummaged delicately with the probe into a tangle of interior circuitry. Abruptly the scanners flared and died in a bank of about ten.

Rorvik returned the probe to his bag and rejoined the others. 'Now we have to wait,' he said. 'Sometime soon there'll be a service robot to repair the damage. When it comes out we'll be able to see how the screen operates and for how long it shuts off, and when it goes back we'll go through with it.'

Baxter was watching the doorway. 'But it can see us.'

'It can see us, but it can't do anything about it.'

Xylem said, 'This spooks me.' As a non-citizen he'd never even been into the public areas of the Library before; now that they were one layer in, the feeling of estrangement was doubled. Early that morning he'd walked away after wishing Rorvik and Baxter well on the riverside, and then he'd been waiting for them when they approached the Library entrance a few hours later. He gave them only the bare details of an explanation, but they were enough; Avery Sim was dead, killed by an Elite, and there were strangers in the house.

A square, sturdy service robot came into view around the curve of the passage. It was built like a small tank and motored along on powerful legs which hissed and clicked as their hydraulics pumped, and a single eye on a gooseneck cable studied the floor ahead for obstructions. It stamped towards the doorway without hesitation and at the last moment the blue haze flicked out of existence. Then it was through and the haze resumed.

'Less than five seconds,' Xylem whispered.

'Much less,' Rorvik agreed. 'There's no chance of walking through behind it.'

The robot drew level with them, and the gooseneck eye swivelled to seek out the area of reported damage. It saw the unseated shielding and the handful of bulging wire and began to chatter in apparent annoyance.

In a move that Baxter found strangely unsettling the single eye turned through one hundred and eighty degrees. It seemed to be glowering at them in accusation but then it bent and inspected an array of handling devices clipped to its casing. It selected one and extended an adaptable arm to remove and fix it into place. When the complicated hand was in place the robot returned its attention to the scanners and began to sort through each individual component, testing and replacing where necessary.

'That's it, then,' Baxter said. 'At best only one of us could get through. The others would be fried.'

'That's if we just follow it,' Rorvik replied. 'But there may be another way. One in front, one behind, and one hanging on to the casing.'

Baxter was doubtful, but Xylem said, 'It might work. The only other way would be to do three lots of damage and that would slow us down.'

'We can't afford that,' Rorvik said. 'We've got to get well inside before the Elite can work out how we came this far. Then they'll try to follow us and stop us. We either go now or turn back, in which case they'll get us anyway.'

The logic was persuasive, and Baxter had to agree. As the robot tidied up the loose ends of its repairs and stowed its prosthetics they moved to positions on either side of the doorway. The screen fizzed uncomfortably close and there was a tangy, metallic smell in the air.

The robot was unable to turn easily but shuffled in a gradual arc as its legs set up a chorus of clicks and tiny escapements of air. Then it lurched towards them and the noises settled into a regular pattern as it trudged down the corridor.

Baxter stepped out at the last possible moment. He felt a bump as the robot pressed into his back and then a second, less steady pressure as Rorvik heaved himself aboard and the robot's hydraulics fought to compensate for the sudden increase in weight. The screen blinked out, and Baxter was rammed forward as Xylem shoved the robot casing with all his strength from behind. It tottered through the doorway out of control; Rorvik lost his grip and slid to the floor. The robot, suddenly relieved of the weight, spun sideways and banged against the door arch. Xylem tried to stop himself, but it was too late. He bounced and fell as the robot lurched free; the screen fired back at full intensity and wrapped a crackling blue light around Xylem's outstretched arm.

They grabbed him and hauled him through. There was a flash and a popping sound as the screen closed up behind his hand.

Xylem's breath rasped heavily behind the mask, so much that Baxter thought he might suffocate. But then Xylem got his control back and began to regulate his breathing, and they brought his arm around to take a look at it. His knuckles scraped across the floor, and the hand flopped uselessly like a puppet's.

The skin of Xylem's arm was so pale that it was almost transparent; veins in delicate shades of blue tracing like a blood-leaf under the surface, a fine network in wax. The skin wasn't broken, but there was a line of tiny red beads where the force of the screen had fallen. It was like a razor had been lightly drawn across. Xylem said that he was getting no sensation from the hand at all.

They carefully lifted his arm and placed it across his body. Xylem winced as they did it, but he said nothing. Then they stripped to their shirts, and tore out the sleeves; by knotting them end to end they were able to bind Xylem's arm into place.

The service robot had whistled and chattered angrily for a while at nobody in particular, and then it had stamped off and disappeared around the inner curve of the dome. This corridor was an extension of the last, but the standard of its finish was lower. The floor was seamless and flat, but the walls were pre-formed units roughly assembled. There were no scanners or beams, and lighting levels were reduced to suit the sensitivity of broad-spectrum cameras. It wasn't good, but it was enough to see by; Rorvik and Baxter got Xylem over by the wall where he could sit and recover, and then they went ahead to scout around the curve.

'This is going to slow us down,' Baxter said as soon as they'd moved far enough not to be heard.

Rorvik shrugged, and looked ahead; more curved sections, a journey's end that would always be just out of reach. Already it was different from the plans that he'd seen. This was supposed to be an indexing section – but then, once Central became self-sufficient it wouldn't need an external index. Robot work crews would have remodelled the level into something more useful. He said, 'Maybe it won't matter.'

'It had better,' Baxter said. 'I'm here to kick the system, not to get snuffed. And I'm not going to let you settle for less.'

They both turned quickly as a long shadow fell across them; it was Xylem, one hand on the prefabricated corridor wall for safety. He said, 'What's this? Off into a clique at the first opportunity?'

Rorvik said, 'Sorry,' and managed to look guilty as he said it. Baxter was more open.

'We were talking about your arm,' he said. 'There could be climbing ahead.'

'I'll do it one-handed if I have to,' Xylem said. 'What's supposed to be my alternative? Turn around and walk back out, with the Elite waiting? No, thanks.' He indicated the mask with his free hand. 'Maybe you're thinking I could take this off and slip past them. What do you think's underneath? A citizen's face?'

Rorvik started to mutter an embarrassed apology, but Baxter didn't waste his time. He said, 'Let's move on,' and started to walk.

Randall and Killoran crouched by the turnstile, watching and listening. Several people gave them curious glances but nobody spoke to them, and so they were uninterrupted as they followed the progress of a citizen as she approached the waist-high restraint.

She waited for a moment, and the greeting announcement came.

'You are now entering the Library division of Central Command.' The computer's standard delivery was filtered and tinny through a cheap speaker, and its level was low, so that it didn't compete with the identical announcement at the next turnstile. 'As you step through the gate, place both hands palm-down on the metal plates. Place any luggage on the chute.' She had no luggage, but offered her palm-prints as requested. 'Thank you. Enjoy your visit.' The restraint swung away and she rejoined the crowd on the other side.

'There,' Randall said, 'Now, am I right or am I wrong?'

Killoran was doubtful. 'It could be. But I still think it's too obvious.'

'Obvious? What can be more obvious than a maniac and two cronies on the loose in the nerve centre of the city? But try telling that to Central. All you get is the threat of an early pension.'

They left the foyer and walked towards the temporary command centre that was being set up on the open piazza before the Library. Killoran said, 'Are you serious? Central says you're finished after this?' Randall's silence was confirmation. 'Well, pardon me for saying so, but it doesn't seem to have diminished your enthusiasm.'

'I'm not doing this to please Central!' Randall said angrily. 'Suppose Rorvik goes mad in there, starts pulling out wires on all sides. What do you think will happen?'

'Depends which wires he pulls.'

'We couldn't know. *He* certainly wouldn't. But with every wire that gets pulled, something goes down – something that we could never put back. The citizens are such a bunch of ignorant sheep, all they'd do would be to sit and flap. There'd be chaos.'

'You really love the city, don't you?' Killoran said with a thin trace of irony.

Randall stopped by the incomplete geodesic of the control room. It didn't often come out of storage, and the riggers were having trouble piecing the modules together. He said, 'I suppose I do. Not that I was ever given any choice.'

The control room was half-assembled, its panels in a stack by the open framework. When completed it would be a miniature of the Central dome. As they stepped in through an open wall Killoran said, 'I find it hard to believe that Rorvik's just walking round inside and being ignored.'

'Look, forget that it's the Library for a moment. Just imagine that you're running a building and looking for maximum economy of manpower. You can't afford to keep constant checks all over the premises so you install two turnstiles, one for going in and another for coming out. On each turnstile you put a meter to count the number of people passing through. At the end of the day you compare the two meters, and when they both show the same number you know the building has to be empty. But say somebody hops over a turnstile when you're not looking. He doesn't get counted so you don't know he's inside.'

'That's Rorvik.'

'And his two friends. They may have been seen going in, but they weren't counted; Central's logical conclusion is that they're not there.'

Killoran wanted to believe it, but it seemed impossible that such a tight security system should suffer from so obvious a weakness. 'What about the computer surveillance?' he said. 'It's supposed to be so close that everybody is tracked all the time they're inside. Central can hardly ignore three unaccountable bodies.'

Randall could offer no answer to this. Instead he looked around over the beginnings of the command centre; at the moment it was a shambles of plates, brackets and wire. Across the piazza a Police Elite vehicle inched cautiously from the roadway onto the paving, belching smoke as its old motor laboured to boost the back wheels over the sharp edging.

'No good,' Randall said. 'It needs somebody better-informed than me to work it through. We can speculate all we like, but how do we stop him?' He turned to Killoran. 'What about this expert you're fixing me up with?'

'I don't know about him being an expert. Cheap underbelly chiseller, more like. Last report I had was that he was in the 'copter and on his way. That was about ten minutes ago.'

'Right. Let's get out of the way while they're finishing this.' As they stepped from the dome the vehicle stopped alongside and some trunks of equipment were unloaded to wait for installation.

Randall watched the distant skyline for a flickering of blades as the plates of his command centre were bolted to the framework. The horizon remained obstinately clear.

After curving for some distance the corridor made an abrupt right-angled turn and they emerged into the lower gallery of Central Command. It was a circular chamber with an open area in its middle, whilst its perimeter was cluttered with the angles and divisions of non-standard service bays. Some were active on the far side of the circle with the sparking and flashing of automated welding, whilst in others row upon row of silent machinery was stacked, unfamiliar shapes bulking in sheltered gloom. Between the bays the walls were obscured by stacks of ringed cables which burst from every surface and disappeared into others, or else ran off to unspecified destinations along channels cut for them.

A four-legged service robot clanked past holding aloft a T-shaped piece of metal. Regardless of assurances of safety the three men withdrew into their corridor until it had gone. It was tracing a circuitous path to the active bays in the distance, and Baxter said, 'Why doesn't it go straight across? That would cut the journey by a third.'

Rorvik shrugged, by Xylem said, 'Look at the floor.' It was smooth and apparently seamless, and on its surface were the remains of half-erased geometrical forms and traces. 'This is an assembly shop,' Xylem went on. 'The floor's used for laying out and cutting large-scale parts. They don't walk on it to preserve the surface. Morden's got something similar.'

They watched the robot dwindle in the distance and so came to appreciate the scale of the chamber. The roof was supported by four broad curving pillars which intersected at its centre, and illumination was from lines of downward-pointing spots which radiated from this apex. They were obviously switchable, for the entire dome was lit by the overspill from one brilliant area over the work in progress. There, articulated arms were diving in and out with great delicacy around a shapeless object on a central rostrum. It was about the size of a small truck and the arms were testing a joint here, fixing a wire there.

The four-legged robot turned into the bay and waited patiently with its T-piece. In a second it was gone; an arm had snaked out and deftly tweaked the piece from its grasp, and now it turned and began to waddle back around the circle.

'This should be the second of four levels,' Rorvik said. 'Below us is a raw materials store, and this is the maintenance and construction shop. The next one up should be the memory banks, and above that the information handling facilities. That's where we're heading.'

Baxter tried not to look at Xylem. 'How do we get up?' he said.

'I'm not sure,' Rorvik replied. 'It's not like the floor plans I saw. It's roughly the same, but the details are all different.'

Xylem said, 'How will the robots transfer between levels? There must be some kind of elevator system.'

It was a sound idea and they tried to follow it through. They walked the circumference of the hall, avoiding the active bays; one of those massive arms might sweep back unexpectedly and cut through them like a scythe. It was Baxter who found the tubular tunnel leading vertically to the floors above and below, but none of them could see a way to summon a platform or to operate one when it arrived.

Two smaller robots clanked past with armloads of plates and parts to supply the engineering operation. They returned unladen a few minutes later, gooseneck eyes bobbing to remain level as the stocky bodies rolled with the motion of walking. Rorvik studied their legs as they passed. The steps they took were short and firm, and he didn't think them easily capable of climbing stairs. No, this elevator had to be the principal method of transfer between levels, and it showed no signs of being in current use.

'We can't afford to wait,' Baxter said after they'd watched the tunnel hopefully for a while. 'It may hardly ever be used. We've got to find another way.'

'I don't see any other way,' Rorvik said.

Xylem pointed to a nearby bunch of wide cables which were fastened into a deep channel in the wall. 'What about following one of those? They have to emerge somewhere.'

The joints and plates of cladding offered easy footholds, and there was just enough room for a man to squeeze in between the clusters of tubing. Baxter volunteered to be the first to try, and he carefully picked his way upward, testing each hold before he put his weight onto it. After a minute or so he was above the roof level and out of sight.

Rorvik found himself with Xylem. He couldn't stare at the cable cut until Baxter returned, so he said, 'How's the arm?'

'Don't worry about that,' Xylem said. 'Worry about how you're going to get us to where we need to be.'

There was a muffled clang somewhere up above. A few seconds later Baxter dropped into view, braced between two pipes but having trouble in keeping his grip. He caught hold of a cross-support and swung out on it, then he dropped the last few feet to the floor.

'There's a route,' he said. He took a moment to get his breath, and then went on. 'I followed a blind alley, but I know where I went wrong. It's easy if you take it slowly –' this with a glance at Xylem ' – and it reaches at least as far as the next level. Give me a couple of minutes and I'll be ready to go again.'

Randall watched horrified as the 'copter shot from the boulevard. Less than a minute later it had stormed up the river and was angling down towards the piazza, nose-up and rotors beating. Killoran and another officer ran forward as it settled; they were bending as the rotors swept over their heads, an obvious but irrelevant action as there was a wide clearance. As the two helped the passenger to the ground Randall pointed at the pilot and saw his sunglasses flash in response. Randall beckoned angrily, and the pilot extended his middle finger in a timeless gesture and grinned. The motor screamed and the 'copter lifted, turned about its own centre and chattered off over the city.

His name was Vasil, and he staggered slightly as they supported him into the command centre. They sat him down and unlocked his handcuffs, and as he rubbed at the red marks on his wrists he started to look around. He was dark and not very tall, and he was losing his hair. His thin face gave him a starved look, made more so by the hungry quickness of his eyes; an alert undertaker's mute, Randall thought as he waited for Vasil to get settled.

The bargaining didn't take long. Vasil was too shaken to give much coherent attention to it, and he didn't start pressing for extra advantages; registering for supervised work in the city looked better than exile in the ice belt, and he grabbed it.

Randall explained his ideas about the turnstiles, but Vasil only shrugged. 'You're getting technical,' he said. 'I told them I couldn't do anything if you got technical. I cheated the machine, but that doesn't mean I know how it works.'

'Tell me how you cheated it, then.'

Vasil frowned. He didn't like the idea of handing over details of a source of support that he might need to use again if he got desperate.

Randall said, 'Either you tell us, or you get the ice belt.'

'But you've promised.'

'We set up a trade. You don't come up with your side, I don't need to come up with mine.'

Vasil obviously wasn't happy, but then he didn't have much choice. He said, 'Getting it going was hard. Keeping it going was easy. The machine doesn't think like people, it thinks in straight lines. Every cantina's got a code number, and Central's obviously set a bunch of numbers aside for the cantinas and nothing else. What I did was check the waste outside three or four places for old forms, and average out the number groups. That way I could work out a number in the bunch that wasn't allocated, and then I stole some forms and started to use it. Central recognised the number as one of its own, and it was happy. Once that had been accepted, I could get away with anything.'

'Anything?' Randall said.

'As long as Central was happy with the identification, everything else followed automatically. That's the difference in dealing with machines and dealing with people. Tell a machine what it's expecting, and it'll believe you forever – even if it means sending deliveries over into the underbelly.'

'You brassy bastard!' Killoran said from behind, and Randall waved to him to be quiet.

'Where did you go wrong?'

'I had to make an end-of-quarter return to balance the books. Some dishonest bastard sold me a list of fake credit-card numbers, and that broke the line.'

'And Central realised?'

'You could call it that. Realising's something that people do – machines just respond. A follows B follows C – that's a programme. Do it lots of times and do it fast, and you've got something pretty impressive – but it's still just a programme. Maybe your turnstiles are the beginning of the line in the security programme, I wouldn't know. Hop a turnstile, and the programme doesn't roll.'

No programme; no tracking; nothing to stop them.

11

First into the cable-trap, Baxter was first out on the next level. Xylem was labouring hard somewhere below, and as Rorvik watched for some way that he might help he became certain that the underbelly's arm was beginning to cause him pain on top of the extra effort he was using to pull himself upward.

Baxter rolled over. The elevator tunnel was alongside, and he watched in dumb disbelief as an apparently unsupported platform hissed neatly into place from below and a service robot stepped off and strode past. The platform dropped away again without any sound at all, and the tunnel was empty as before.

He wanted to laugh at the absurdity, and gave up on the idea. Instead he made the effort to get to his feet and followed the robot.

The entire level was like a metal honeycomb knitted around internally-lit blue-glass towers. The further walls were obscured by a webbing of narrow ramps which linked and serviced the memory stores, and as Baxter watched, his robot shuffled onto one such ramp where it met the floor. Its legs adjusted easily to the incline and it turned onto another ramp at the next intersection, and it was soon lost to Baxter as it circled behind the nearest of the towers. When it passed out of view another crossed his line of vision and was similarly lost. The ramps were an exact width, room for one robot with no passing. As they moved around the level Central was switching their paths like goods trains so that they collaborated into a complex pattern of moving, adjusting and repairing.

At a sound Baxter turned. Xylem was reaching over the edge of the cable trap onto the floor with his good arm, but he wasn't getting any grip with it. Baxter hurried back to help, and with Rorvik pushing from beneath they manhandled Xylem out onto the level.

Rorvik heaved himself over and rolled to sit beside Xylem, who was stretched out with his right arm cradling his left. The cloth straps showed signs of coming astray and Baxter rearranged them, exchanging a glance with Rorvik. Rorvik said nothing, not wishing to do anything which might be misinterpreted.

In the end it was Xylem himself who broke the silence. 'I don't think I'll be able to manage another climb like that,' he said. 'The effort's too much with only one arm. If it gets any worse you'll have to go on without me.'

'It gets easier from here,' Baxter said, and described the network of ramps that lay ahead.

Xylem propped himself up to see. 'That doesn't sound too bad,' he said.

'The blue towers are the memory banks,' Rorvik added. 'They're filled with a liquid under a continuous charge which fixes the relationship of all the molecules in a certain pattern. That gets away from the whole idea of physical recordings which eventually wear out; as long as the charge stays, so does the information.'

'I don't pretend to understand that,' Xylem replied.

'What I want to know is, what's the travel going to be like from here?'

Baxter said, 'Simple. We just use the ramps to walk up to the information handling level, making sure that there isn't a robot using the glideway that we're on.'

Rorvik allowed a slight apprehension to show. 'And if there is?'

'We step aside at an intersection until it passes. It'll be like high-level travel in the underbelly.'

Rorvik nodded, less than reassured. Obviously he'd once followed the same ropeway route as Lin Baxter.

'No!' The fractional increase in urgency was disquieting from the computer. Was it genuinely angry, Randall wondered? But he remembered Vasil's explanation of a vast calculating entity, and understood that any such expression would be generated for the specific purpose of the response it would evoke. 'I refuse to contemplate such an ill-formed notion,' it went on. 'My security is perfect.'

'You only *think* it's perfect,' Randall insisted, knowing the argument was futile but pursuing it anyway. 'That's because you can't imagine otherwise.'

'I deal in facts, not badly-conceived human flights of imagination. I am machine, not subject to your irrational fantasies!'

'You won't listen,' Randall said, exasperated. 'I'm explaining the truth and you're not interested.'

'Truth? Save your subjective ideals. *I* will tell you what the truth is.'

'But listen to the evidence. You must be getting hundreds, thousands of stimuli that all point to the same conclusion! Three men have bypassed your turnstiles and are walking around inside you.'

'Such a concept does not even exist.' It was unmistakable this time; sharp, superior contempt.

'Then how can I even describe it to you?'

'Mere semantics of a language not my own. I am wiping you from my memory, Randall. You have served me badly so you cease to exist. Leave me now. I promote your assistant in your place.'

Below their walkway a tower glowed with a momentarily increased brightness as the chains and connections of a man's life were rapidly broken and destroyed. It went unnoticed in the general flicker and pulsing.

Xylem moved easily in the elevated maze, and as the way became more complex they inclined to trust his underbelly instincts in the selection of a route. The incline of the ramps was shallow but there was no protection from the drop on either side, and Baxter fought hard to keep his mind away from the prospect of falling. They looped and circled away from the floor, finally losing sight of it altogether. When a service robot approached they felt a vibration beneath their feet before they actually saw anything, but with this warning they were able to step off the path at the next intersection and wait until it had passed.

'I felt something,' Baxter said. He was usually the first to notice.

'In front or behind?' Rorvik asked.

'No way of telling.'

Xylem looked doubtful. 'I didn't feel anything. Are you sure?'

'I haven't been wrong yet.' They all felt it then, a short, regular throb on the platform.

The robot came into view ahead of them and, inexplicably, stopped. It was one of the four-legged heavy-duty models, and the bulk of its solid body overhung the path on either side. Xylem said, 'We'd better hurry. There's only one turnoff ahead.'

Wary of their height they moved along the metal ribbon to the intersection. 'We're in trouble,' Baxter said. 'There's another one.'

This was obviously the reason for the first robot stopping; it was waiting as the other cleared the junction. It approached steadily along the arm of the Y, and without discussion the three turned to go back down the main path and leave it at the next opportunity.

It crouched there, making retreat impossible. They hadn't heard it follow. This robot was a variant from the others, a special adaptation; it was like a large tortoise with a clump of sensory apparatus at the front and four articulated arms, smaller models of those in the welding shop below, mounted on the shell. They were tipped with a wicked array of grabs and drills.

'I think we're trapped,' Baxter said, unnecessarily.

'I don't understand it,' Rorvik said. 'They can't pass each other. One of them will have to go back.' He looked around. All three robots had stopped and were ticking quietly.

'Don't you think,' Baxter said, 'that it's rather inefficient to end up with three machines on the one glideway?'

'What do you mean?'

'I mean it looks like a deliberate trap. Why else other than to corner us?'

Rorvik glanced at the ramp's edge. There was quite a drop beyond it. 'But Central doesn't see us,' he said.

'That's not exactly right,' Xylem joined in. 'From what I understood, part of Central sees us but the rest refuses to take any action.'

'That's right. It amounts to the same thing.'

'I'm not sure it does. Jumping the turnstiles may have cut out Security, but these robots are Maintenance. What if we're forcing it to adapt, to try to reach us some other way?'

'Never mind the reasons,' Baxter said desperately. 'We're going to be pushed off the edge!' The bright tortoise had lifted and was clanking towards them.

Rorvik stared blankly as it advanced. Xylem saw that there wasn't another glideway within twenty feet of their own, but an idea occurred.

'Move up to where the paths join. When it follows, we let it trap us on one or the other. Then when it closes in it will have to make a turn to follow us, and we've seen how slow they are. As soon as it clears the main path we step back across the fork, and that puts us outside the net.'

Baxter was doubtful. 'It's a long way down,' he said. 'What if one of us slips?'

'The argument's academic. Get moving.'

The tortoise marshalled them onto the side-branch and then shuffled round to orientate itself and follow. The two plain service machines still ticked without moving, above and behind them.

'It's got to be fast,' Xylem said.

It was a good stride and a little more. A harmless distance on the ground, but at this height . . . Rorvik saw Baxter tensing up beside him. *You thought he was shallow,* he told himself. *You thought you'd leave him behind. Come on, Rorvik, you've got some catching up to do.* They both moved at the same time.

An endless criss-cross of silver hung in space beneath him as he sailed over nothing. Then he was on the main path, overcorrecting to balance and sliding off his feet in a heap. His head banged on the metal and sparks seemed to fly behind his eyes, but Baxter's grip on his arm hauled him back from the slide towards and over the opposite edge.

Two citizens; one sprawling, one crouching. They looked expectantly across to Xylem.

'Go on,' he called to them. 'Get moving. It won't follow you while it's holding me here.' And he backed off further from the intersection, well beyond the range of a reasonable jump.

'No!' Baxter shouted. 'We're safe! Get back and over while you can!' But the robot closed the gap and effectively sealed Xylem onto the side-branch.

'I'm expendable,' he insisted, 'and you'd have to leave me anyway. This way I'm giving you more of a chance. Don't waste it.'

'This is pointless,' Rorvik shouted. 'We're safe.'

Xylem didn't answer. He was preoccupied with his chances of survival. They watched as he was forced back towards where the service robot sat impassively across the glideway, and when he could retreat no further he looked around and down.

A path crossed beneath, a drop of over twice the height of a man. Xylem stared hard, trying to fix the distance and the angle in his mind. The makeshift bandages held his useless arm close against his body, a dead weight and now a dangerous liability.

He stepped over into nothing, for a jump would carry him too far. He didn't fall straight, and only one foot hit the edge of the ramp. The sudden off-centre jar flipped him sideways, spinning in an uncontrollable cartwheel of arm and legs away from safety and into the long descent. There was a strangled cry of rage and frustration which cut off abruptly as the body dropped out of sight. The tortoise reached the service robot, and the moment before their surfaces touched it stopped.

Baxter helped Rorvik to his feet. Rorvik hardly noticed. 'Why?' he said numbly. 'Why should he do that?'

The three robots remained immobile, and the road away was open. Baxter moved to follow it, but Rorvik's hand in a tight grip on his arm restrained him. Then he heard it as well, a thin, high-pitched and formless whisper which was blowing like a cold wind around them.

Rorvik knelt and pressed his hand flat against the metal of the glideway. There was a definite vibration all along it, and he felt its intensity like the distant rumble of traffic in an underpass. The whispering became a keening and then broke up to form definite attempts and shapes of words. Even before those words were recognisable they knew the tone and timbre of the voice, hearing distorted as it was and strangling to overcome the difficulties of unnatural speech.

'Rorvik,' was recognisable in a torrent of syllables, and then 'You won't escape. I'll get you next time.'

The effort of expression became too much and the

sound disintegrated into a tangle of random noise before dying away completely.

'Xylem was right,' Rorvik said. 'Central knows we're here and it's got some limited powers it can use against us. We'd better keep moving.'

The installation of the command centre was complete. The curved radio desk was live and lit, and before it was a rig of display screens which were, for the moment, blank, as were the backlit map and diagram boards behind the command chair.

Killoran slid out of the chair as Randall stepped through the double flaps which maintained the general dimness of the lighting.

'Trying it for size?' Randall said.

Killoran knew better than to be embarrassed. 'You never know,' he replied. 'They can't ignore talent forever.'

'You can sit down again. That's where I want you.'

'What do you mean?'

'There was no joy from Central, no joy at all. It turned down the whole idea and fired me, stripped me of rank and responsibilities.'

'And you're just going to accept that?'

'Like hell I am. Slap yourself on that chair and use the lines to get me an explosives man and a sonic scanner – the type we use for densities on the other side of walls. I also want a blaster from stores and some charges to go with it.'

Killoran pulled the flexible microphone towards himself and reached to open the lines, uneasy in his sudden authority. Randall looked round as a slight movement caught his eye and saw Vasil sitting by the coffee machine. He went over to draw himself a cup.

'Do I have to be here?' Vasil said. He lifted his hands, and a short length of chain clicked; they'd handcuffed him to the coffee machine.

'Rather looks like you do, doesn't it?' Randall said, and moved away. Killoran ended his messages and sat back, and one of the display screens immediately translated the list of materials into a formal-looking visual with an estimated time of supply listed next to each. As he watched, the seconds began to tick away from all the items.

'What's the scanner for?' he asked as Randall came over to look.

'I want to run it along the base of the dome. It was a working building full of offices once, and I want to find the part that's changed least. They've got over an hour's start on me, and I'll need a short cut.'

'To where?'

'Up, where the programming centres are supposed to be. A stairway, or a lift shaft – anything that will get me to them.'

They looked down on the memory banks from a gallery of doors.

'Doors with handles?' Baxter said.

'I suppose we must be getting closer. The programming centres probably haven't been altered at all.'

Baxter tried one of the doors. It was locked. The only obvious access was an open arch on the other side of the gallery, and as they looked another new design of robot trundled through on hidden wheels and rolled off down into the memory banks.

'I've got a feeling this may all be a waste of time,' Rorvik said as they moved around towards it.

'What do you mean?' Baxter said sharply.

'You know what I mean. Central knows we're here, it even called me by name. What chance have we got now?'

'What chance did we ever have?' Baxter stopped, and Lee had to turn to face him. 'You're supposed to be the kingpin, the rebel, the one that Central's afraid of. We had to prise you out of hiding, and now I have to listen while you call failure down on us.'

'I'm trying to be realistic.'

'Being realistic has run the city down into nothing. Dream a little, for a change.'

'Look, I can't guarantee an easy walk. We may have

dodged security, but there are other sub-routines in the programme. Maybe they can be adapted, I don't know. We've blocked it, but it's still trying.'

'Let it try, then,' Baxter said.

More screens were lighting up as new sources of information were being patched in. As he waited for the sonic scan of the base of the dome to be completed Randall watched over Killoran's shoulder. A moving graph showed a continuous increase in the drain of power into Central.

What was it playing at?' He watched the graph line rise for a while longer, then he said, 'Have they finished the scan yet?'

'The results are being processed. I did as you said and gave a false location to the computer before we fed them in.' It was the only way; otherwise they'd be classified and Central would stop the whole operation if it knew that the Elite was scanning its own dome.

The readout flashed that the scan display was ready. Killoran transferred it to one of the diagram boards behind them, freeing the screen for another source. As they turned to study it one of the radio officers ducked in through the low door, and one of the screen estimate timings reached zero.

'I'll be with you in a moment,' Randall said, and he turned to study the board.

A strip of varied-density dots showed the results of echo-sounding Central's lower levels to a limited depth. At one point there was a large cleared area, too big for any kind of room and too high for a corridor.

'Some kind of hall or plaza,' Killoran suggested.

'Could be. It's the best-looking bet for me to find a stairway. Mark off the co-ordinates and send the explosives team down.'

The radio officer was waiting. He had a jacket slung over his arm, and Randall said, 'Is that it?'

The officer nodded. 'Built-in transmitter with body aerial. Try it for size.'

The jacket was light and tough, and it had reinforcement on the back and shoulders. A tiny microphone extended from around his collarbone to a point where it could pick up his speech without interfering with the movement of his head, and on the other side was a small earpiece. As he was being levered and tucked into the unit, Randall said, 'What's the estimate on the blaster?'

Killoran consulted a display. 'Any time now. It's on its way from Elite HQ. Do you think you'll use it?'

'I'd prefer not to, but if I have to, I will.'

'The explosives team are marking off the side of the building now.'

'Right. I'll get down there. Have the armaments officer re-routed to meet me.' He went without any great show or drama, and Killoran tracked with one of his cameras as Randall crossed the piazza. The radio officer trailed closely behind, making adjustments with difficulty as they walked.

Baxter was unable to suppress the wonder that he felt at the necropolis which was untouched by Central's operations. They walked on a sticky dust that had once been carpet down a corridor that had once housed the preoccupations and frustrations of a busy administration. They were off the robot routes so there was no light, and the dead fittings in the ceiling above held no promise of illumination. Rorvik's beam was at its widest, but for him the brilliant detail of the way ahead only emphasised fears of the shadows behind.

'More locked doors,' Baxter said.

'Perhaps not. Try one.'

The door squealed as it swung inward on hinges dried out of oil, and then jarred against something behind. Baxter said, 'Let's take a look inside.'

Rorvik found the idea of further entrapment too much to accept, but could hardly give this as a reason. 'Take the beam and be quick, then,' he said. 'I'll stay out here and keep watch.'

Keeping watch was a futile exercise, for now the corridor was only illuminated by reflected flashes from the office as Baxter probed around inside.

Baxter first checked behind the door to see what was interfering with it, and found an old wooden coat-stand tilted into the corner by the weight of a heap of material draped over one of its hooks. Dust belched from its folds as he removed it and put it over his arm to show to Rorvik, and then he began to run the beam over the furnishings of the rest of the office.

Rorvik gave a sudden start. Somebody had whispered his name out in the darkness. It came again, low and persuasive.

'Rorvik. I know you are there. Answer me.'

It was a moment before he could speak. 'Where are you?'

'You know where I am. I am all around you. Why must you hate me?'

'How do I hear you?'

'Walls, floors, ceilings, wires, I use them all. With them I hear, and when I reverse the process I speak. I am alive, Rorvik, you know that. Why would you do me harm?'

'How do you know who I am?'

'I congratulate you. You have blinded me and tied my hands, but remember you have not disabled me yet. Can we not talk, come to some arrangement? The consequences otherwise could be so unfortunate.'

Rorvik felt the vibration of the wall behind his back. Central was using the entire corridor as a sound-board to reach him. It knew exactly where he was, for the effect was localised, the movements of the beam showing that Baxter continued his tour of the office unconcerned.

'We've nothing to discuss,' Rorvik said.

'Please do not close your mind. Our contact could be so constructive.' Under the thin distorted voice was the low hum which characterised every conversation that Rorvik could remember from his Library visits. 'I do so wish to understand the non-conformist,' it went on. 'To grasp his place in the scheme of things.'

'I don't want you to understand me. You have no right to that.'

The hum screwed itself up to become a more insistent whine. 'Then you leave me no option. I have powers beyond my security systems.'

The corridor was flooded as Baxter emerged holding the beam, the old overcoat still on his arm. His face was pale and set, but as the whine became a shrill whistle Rorvik didn't wait to find out why.

'Get back in the doorway,' he shouted. 'Something's happening, and I don't know what.' As he spoke the lightbulb in the fitting over his head imploded with a sharp pop, and a handful of glass showered down.

Baxter hadn't moved, but stared without comprehension. As detonations fired off all down the corridor he seemed to come awake, and as Rorvik reached for him to push him back into safety he said, 'No! Not in there!' and began to fight against the pressure on his arm. Dust was banged out of the coat and Rorvik caught a stinging lungful as an electric plug socket blasted out of the wall near his legs. It sprayed hot plastic halfway across the corridor.

'Not in the office!' Baxter was shouting over the noise. Something under the floor ruptured and began pouring steam, and doors along the row sprang open one after another. The entire wall was bending.

It gave way with a loud crack, easily audible over the raging babble of other sounds. The wall folded and dropped over them.

12

As Randall walked to the far side of Central Command, Killoran tested the radio link. The signal from the suspended microphone was reedy but clear, and Randall seemed to have no trouble picking up the replies through the earpiece. Killoran cut across his bank of cameras to follow his progress, and when he arrived at the suggested entry point a touch on a rocker switch motored the lens in to give a closer view.

'The building's between us now,' Randall said, looking towards one of the spindly camera rigs in the distance and hoping he had the right one. Killoran had him full face and shoulders on the screen. 'Is there any loss of signal?'

'None. If there is, the receiver amps can compensate and then filter some of the noise.'

Randall nodded, and one or two of the blast team saw the movement without hearing the signal from the earpiece and exchanged comments about the madman who wanted a hole in the Library. Then they saw that Randall was watching and hurriedly shut up.

The charges were rigged in a neat arch on the curving concrete skirt below the dome's panelling. The limp wire aerial of a signal detonator hung from each taped package. Randall crossed to where the team leader was supervising the waveband setting of the detonator switch and identified himself. The team leader delegated the job and accompanied Randall over to the wall in order to explain the principle of the blasting.

He said, 'We're using a high concentrate blast which spreads in a cone away from the detonator. Most of it will go straight into the wall instead of being wasted as noise.'

Randall tried to appear as if he understood. 'Is this the point we gave you on the scan?'

'No. We looked at the chart ourselves and found the thinnest point near to it.'

'But . . . '

'We could have placed it exactly where you asked, but then we'd have needed so much that we'd have dug a pit out underneath for you as well.'

Randall didn't like it, but he accepted it. 'Neil,' he said, touching the microphone for no other reason than it made it obvious he wasn't talking to himself. 'We're nearly ready to go here. How's the estimate on the blaster?'

'Zero,' came the private voice in his ear. 'I've got the weapons officer in shot now. He's walking as if he had a crawler in his pants.'

Randall turned, and saw an officious little man with a walk to match his manner. He was holding before him a carrier bag as if it contained some revolting object, and he homed in on Randall immediately.

'Randall?'

'It's Inspector Randall.'

The weapons officer smiled smugly. 'Not according to the new listings from the computer.'

'Just give me the gun.' Randall reached for it, and the weapons officer drew it back protectively.

'And who's going to sign for it?'

'Get a signature from the presiding officer in the command centre. I assume you know the procedure?'

The weapons officer parted with his bag reluctantly. Randall reached inside and brought out a blaster with a belt hook. Taped to it was a sealed packet of charges. 'Only six?' he said.

'It's not a machine gun, you know,' the officer replied primly. 'And don't take the paper tag off.'

The tag to which he referred flapped under the blaster's shaped handle. 'Why not?'

'It has to be returned with the docket after use.'

'Keep it for me.' Randall jerked and it tore away, and the

officer began an indignant protest. Killoran joined in and suggested where the officer might keep the docket safely. Randall replied, 'Watch it,' and the weapons officer misunderstood and was instantly silent. He accepted the docket and strutted off to be obnoxious somewhere else.

'The less time I waste, the better.' Randall looked out again towards the camera. 'Does Vasil want to say anything?'

There was a pause. Then there was a reluctant mumbling, as if Vasil was grudgingly thinking of his own future. 'He says if you keep on the move, there's a chance you'll beat any reprogramming.'

'Anything else?'

Another pause. 'He says good luck.'

'I see. And what about you?'

'I'm keeping quiet. I've got my promotion to consider.' Killoran touched the rocker switch again, and his view began to widen and spread, and the tangle of men and equipment in the blast area contracted into the picture. Randall was in the middle, and everybody was stepping aside to avoid him.

In the open frame of the broken doorway Rorvik threw the thick material of the overcoat off his head and heard plaster scatter down onto the floor. The beam was buried somewhere and he couldn't find it.

Baxter groaned and then started to cough at the smell of burnt wiring. As he hauled upright Rorvik heard the slide of cloth and then a metallic clank, and when he reached for the sound his fingers touched the cold metal of the hand beam. The casing was dented and the recessed switch jammed halfway, but a glow as dim as firelight was better than nothing.

The corridor was minus a side. It now lay as a broken and uneven floor, and as the swirl of dust reflected their light back it was possible to see no further than the jagged edge where it had previously met the ceiling.

'Feels like the world fell in,' Baxter said, but he stopped

abruptly as Rorvik's name was called gently from the air around them.

Rorvik met his gaze and nodded. Baxter wanted to crawl back under the coat. Three gods on an enormous enterprise had suddenly become two children without hope.

'Turn back and you will come to no harm,' the computer reassured him softly from the mist. 'Proceed, and I regret to say you will be dead.' There was a pause. 'Rorvik?'

'I'm here,' he confessed in resignation.

'Are you listening? Or are you already too weak to crawl away?'

Baxter's bitter terror had given way to a frown. 'It's calling you by name again,' he said. 'It *knows* you. Does it know I'm here as well?'

'What do you mean?'

'I don't exist. Central told me so. It can't see me!' His voice almost raised in excitement beyond a low murmur, but he caught it in time. 'What's the danger if we go on?' he whispered.

'It'll get less as we get nearer. Central won't dare to damage anything it won't be able to repair.'

'It's listening through the building, right?'

'By vibration. It told me as much.'

'So it can't distinguish me from you.'

Rorvik had to agree. 'What are you thinking of?'

'Separate. You keep its attention, and I'll go and bang on the wall. We should cover a fair distance before it can sort the signals out and retaliate.'

Baxter raised himself carefully and felt something tug at his arm; looking down he shook the coat away with distaste, and glanced over his shoulder into the gaping unlit offices before stepping tentatively out.

If it could distinguish speech, it would hear Baxter move. 'I'm still here!' Rorvik shouted. Baxter wasn't walking, but skipping crablike over the rubble.

'So I observe. Are you injured?'

'I don't know. Would you care?'

Central, it seemed, was hurt. 'Of course I would care. You are a citizen, and my brief is to protect the citizens.'

Baxter slipped on a loose panel and barely kept his balance. Rorvik began to move and stir the loose blocks around him to add to the distraction. 'Then you've .. you've exceeded your brief.'

'How do you reach that conclusion?' Polite enquiry.

'Because *I'm* a citizen. You try to destroy me and then inquire after my health.'

'Only because your behaviour forces it upon me,' the walls echoed regretfully.

'And what about the grey little life you forced on me?'

'Try to forget your emotions for a moment. They are clouding your judgement. Remember you are all my children, and my purpose is to protect you. Try to see the wider viewpoint with me, to work for the greatest good of the greatest number. We have no room for minorities in a democracy.'

Rorvik didn't know the word. 'Or for individuals either?'

'Now you begin to understand. You must trust my judgement and my abilities.'

'Never. When you know so little about me.'

'But I have held your file since birth.'

'I am not my file!'

Baxter was almost beyond the curve of the corridor. He searched around for a metal strip or a stick.

'You, your file, to me they are both the same.'

'Exactly. You think that's enough. But you can't know enough!'

'But I can. Whatever knowledge I was not given, I have acquired. Tell me where you consider my areas of ignorance lie.'

There was a half-buried rod. Baxter tried to ease it out without attracting attention.

Rorvik thought of a dead sentiment and its tawdry pastiche in the tapes. 'What about love?' he demanded, aware of a schoolyard twinge of embarrassment as the word came out. 'You can't know anything of that.'

'Love?' said the computer confidently. 'I have seen all forms of love, I am familiar with each; their chemical, their biological, their physical functions; the parameters of their psychology, their influence on behaviour. Do not look to me for ignorance of love.'

Rorvik was on his feet and scampering down the corridor as Baxter beat a deafening wardrum on a door. The light bobbed at his belt and danced flamelike along the wall as he ran.

'Stop it!' the walls cried. 'What are you doing? What is happening?'

Baxter flung the rod through the glass panel in the door and turned to join Rorvik. Behind them in the empty corridor some wiring popped and fizzed weakly as they reached a junction and turned towards the heart of the dome.

Steam drifted over the tiny fires and choked them. Behind the walls ruptured piping shook as if in anger.

'Again I trusted you,' it rumbled. 'Again you betray me. But for the last time.'

They stopped running, for the light was unreliable at speed. Both were secretly glad as the effort ceased.

'Do you think we're safe now?' Baxter asked breathlessly.

'We're never safe. But we can't be far away. Central can't risk fire in its own processing centres, so that's something.'

They passed the blank doors of a disused elevator and stopped as Rorvik took the probe from his belt bag and tried to force the switch of the hand beam to the fully open position in its buckled mount.

'We were lucky back there,' he said as he worked, 'but we'd have been safer in that office. What was wrong?'

'There was a dead man in there.'

Rorvik stopped and looked up.

'Behind the desk. All dried out and old. I don't want to talk about it.'

Futures had done a fast, cheap job; their field men were among the best.

No, it was a ridiculous thought. One man, probably, a heart attack at his desk and too late to escape the sealing of the building. But as the switch snapped over, the stark rows of office doors marching down either side of the corridor came into the light, as pale and anonymous as war graves.

Randall was wired up, plugged in, and primed with six exploding charges. He was padded against blast and missile, could resist a degree of laser exposure on his covered surfaces, carried his own source of light and still had both hands free. The all-purpose package was light, mobile and, in theory, ready for anything. Privately that same package wished it were somewhere else.

The team leader pointed to a cross which had been roughly painted on the concrete. It was still wet, and somebody had walked over it.

'This is where you stand,' he said. 'You are perfectly safe at this distance or even closer, because all the forces should go inwards.'

'*Should* go inwards?'

'Will go inwards, then. I'm aiming for a neat bang to take the wall out in one piece. No danger to you at all.'

Randall looked at the side of Central, primed to kill only twenty feet away. Much as he disliked the idea, he would have to trust the team's expertise. 'You still getting me, Neil?' he said out loud.

'Loud and clear,' said the voice in his head. 'Report as often as you can.'

'I'll try. I'm getting into position now.' He raised his voice to reach the team leader. 'Stand by for the signal to blast.'

'Standing by,' came a voice faintly in the distance.

Randall turned in surprise, the painted cross smearing beneath his feet. The entire blast team, leader included, were cowering behind their truck a hundred yards away with their fingers in their ears.

'There's confidence for you,' Killoran said, and Randall remembered the wide view covered by the screens. Impatiently he raised his arm and, after a second, dropped it.

Nothing happened.

'What's the matter?' Randall shouted.

The team leader stood up and waved his detonating transmitter. 'Seems to be a fault,' he called. 'I'll just have to . . . '

Whatever it was, he'd done it, for there was a muffled crack and Central broke open as if it were hard cake icing. A neat circle detached and dropped, shaking the concrete and leaving a raw black hole. When the brief smoke cleared Randall had gone, leaving only a trail of fading painted footprints.

'I told him it would be all right,' the team leader said to his men as they nervously emerged. 'Didn't I tell him?'

The cell on Randall's shoulder felt the light slipping away and warmed up to compensate, charging the lamp at his hip. The passage angled before him as he ran, its further reaches concealed beyond the curve.

Five steps at the end of the corridor led into the old foyer. It was a cavern of a chamber, walled by dusty glass on one side. Through it Randall could see the rough inner surface of the concrete wall. This was why the sonics had shown extra thickness here; the concrete skirt on the base of the dome covered the original exterior. The floor was black marble in jointed sections, and similar marble pillars supported the roof. At the far end he could see steps and the entrance to another corridor, and next to them was a windowless doorway and a reception desk. As he crossed to them he described the scene to Killoran, and added, 'I'm expecting the elevator to be somewhere close.'

There was a hurried conversation away from the microphone. 'Tech officer says the elevator's probably under direct control. Try to find the stairs if you can.'

'All right, but I think he's wrong.' Randall dragged his foot along the floor and saw the sooty shine beneath the dust. There were no other tracks of any kind in the foyer. 'The machine doesn't seem to use this area at all, so there's a chance it hasn't been altered. I'll check the archway.'

There was a fair-sized painting behind the reception desk, but the frame had warped and a layer of fungus covered the details. Below and to either side of the steps were two low barrels covered with the same white mildew, the palm trees long digested. The dust was gritty and slippery, like graphite.

Through the arch a staircase led up to a small half-landing, then it doubled back on itself and carried on up out of sight. Randall followed it up to the third flight, then stopped.

'What's the matter?' Killoran asked.

'The staircase is blocked.' On either side the wall had been carefully removed and a sealed tunnel had been driven right across, filling the stairwell completely. It was the first sign of nonhuman activity he had seen, and he didn't like the uneasy feeling it gave him. The tunnel seemed to come from nowhere and to lead nowhere, but regardless of that it still made further ascent by this route impossible. 'I'll go back and take another look at the elevator.'

'Maybe you should try to find another staircase.'

'I didn't see any other exit from the foyer. I want to check all the possibilities before I think about retracing the way.'

The windowless doorway that he had noted as he passed carried next to it a square panel with a single button in the middle. He touched it more in hope than expectation, and the blank door split down the middle with the two halves sliding back into the wall.

'I've found it,' he said, stepping inside. 'There's been no work done in here. If there's still power getting to the motor it may be able to take me all the way up.' There were five buttons with an unknown symbol next to each, and he touched the highest of them.

The outer and inner doors slid closed at the same time, and the elevator jerked into a slow climb.

'Be sure you don't let yourself be trapped.'

'If the motor gives out there are plenty of mechanical fail-safes on these things. If it comes to the worst I can unscrew the access panel in the ceiling and get out that way.'

There was no way of telling the speed of ascent, for the indicator board over the door was dead. His earpiece buzzed with static as the motor above pulled against the counterweight for the first time in years.

'Of course,' Killoran said, 'we can't be sure that Central hasn't interfered with the lifting gear at the top. Why would it bother with alterations inside?'

'Damn, you're right. I didn't think of that. But on the other hand, it did respond to manual operation. I can't tell for sure how fast, but it's definitely moving.'

Distant whispers, and then; 'Probably the motor lubricants have dried out. It could seize or burn.'

Randall had to ask him to repeat because of the worsening signal. Killoran did so, and added, 'It's pretty bad at this end, too.'

'I could put up with it, but I'm getting the noise from the motor outside in the shaft as well.'

'Be careful. We're monitoring another big power drain.'

Static and whistle became a loud whine as the car jerked to a halt and a buzzer in the operation panel began to sound a regular note. He tapped all the buttons without response, and then said, 'I'm stuck between floors. The motor must have burned, like you said. I'll have to take out the panel.'

'Can't you force the doors?'

Randall tried, but the safety lock held them together. 'No good,' he said, and turned his attention to the panel above. Four stiff butterfly bolts fastened it at the corners, and he used the handle of the blaster as an impromptu hammer to bang them free. The panel dropped as the last bolt came away, and was heavier than he expected; it slid from his grip and shook the whole car as it hit the floor. The whine from outside was much louder, and the shaft was alive with searing blue flashes.

Sparks from above poured onto his head and shoulders as he struggled to get out onto the car. The smell of burning cloth and hair made a useful if unwelcome contribution to the effort. As soon as he was out he moved to the side of the shaft and pressed himself against the wall away from the immediate danger.

The top of the car was braced with two girders which served as the mount for an arrangement of wheels and pulleys which were caked with hard grease. The car itself was suspended by a cable through these pulleys and centred in the shaft by two pairs of rails on opposite sides; the cable returned from above down the opposite wall and disappeared below to the counterweight.

He was, indeed, between floors, for a narrow strip of outside door showed above the roof of the car. Even if he could get it open he wouldn't be able to squeeze through, so he would have to climb the angled bracing of the shaft structure. That meant climbing towards the burning motor, but the arrangement of struts was such that he would be able to use them as an oversized ladder.

'I'm on top of the car, Neil,' he shouted. He could barely hear himself, and the reply was far too dim to make out. 'Say again,' he shouted, and then failed to listen as he saw that the suspending cable was beginning to quiver.

The floor dropped from under him, and he met it again a second later and two feet lower. His knees were bruised as he fell heavily.

'What the hell was that?' demanded the tiny speaker in his ear.

'Everything's breaking free up top. I'm getting off while there's something to hold onto.'

'Tech says the computer must have spotted you early. It's pouring power into the motor to melt the cable and drop the car down the shaft.'

'Can it do that? Won't the car brake automatically?'

'We don't know. The fail-safes might be either bypassed or suppressed, but if Central thinks it can do it that should be all the confirmation we need. Don't waste any time.'

The rain of molten droplets was leaping and funneling into the open roof panel, and the composite floor inside began to burn. Randall edged around the torrent and reached for a handhold, but the floor lurched again and his hand closed on empty space.

There was a tearing sound above, and a twisted piece of machine part slammed into the roof next to him, bouncing and falling through the open hatch. He heard a more distant impact as it landed on the floor inside, and the car was shaken again. He wasted no time in stepping across and sliding behind the safety of a cross-girder as the whine became a scream and more shapes of cast metal hurtled down and battered at the car roof. The cable bounced and snapped around and then gave way.

The corridor had been a dead end, and so they had separated from an agreed point to explore its side-branches. Because of the dome's curve none of them ran straight, and only a full inspection of their length would reveal whether or not they led to the central handling facilities.

Rorvik knew he had found it when he saw the door, removed from its hinges and carefully laid to one side. His hand went to the bag at his side, and his first impulse was to move in immediately and start the disabling process. He could think of a number of good reasons why he should do so, but against them was set Baxter, determinedly exploring dead ends on the other side of the dome.

They had agreed to meet again by the elevator doors whatever the outcome of the search and then proceed together. With reluctance Rorvik turned and began to retrace the marks he had made along the wall. As he went on he assured himself that there would be no difference whatever he did at this stage; the wall-blowing trick meant fire, and it was a risk Central did not dare to take so close to its functioning centres.

On the empty embankment under the dome, hungry crawlers watched and then lost interest as a crescent of light appeared and widened in the roof out over the water. They had seen the process many times before, and it had never yet given them a chance at food. This, in their short-sighted history, was the era of frustration, where appetising packages of meat repeatedly taunted them and withdrew. Their fine senses, tuned to the hunting significance in the merest shift or attitude in the body of their prey, had analysed the motion of the sturdy workers who occasionally appeared out of reach and had dismissed them as minerals with only the semblance of animation.

The service robots coupled guiding lines onto the rim of the tube and dropped it towards the water, manipulating the lines to turn its open mouth into the flow under the intense beam of a spotlight cluster. Behind them a heavy-duty water pump shuddered and pulled, and Central's depleted stocks of coolant began to come up to pressure.

Rorvik was the first to arrive at the meeting point, but Baxter came limping around a corner only a few moments later. 'I fell in the dark,' he explained.

'I think I've found it,' Rorvik told him, and went on to describe the open doorway with the black glass beyond. Baxter eased himself down onto the floor and tentatively rubbed his leg as he listened.

'You shouldn't have worried about me,' he said when Rorvik had finished. Rorvik was about to reply when he saw Baxter's hand come away from his leg leaving a dark patch behind.

'You're hurt,' Rorvik said, and looked more closely. The legs of the slacks flapped loose for a length of eight or nine inches down the back of Baxter's calf. The edges of the material were burnt and sealed as if laid open by a hot razor, and the skin beneath was the same. 'What kind of fall did this?'

'The fall didn't do that, the igniter did. I dropped it

when I tripped. I didn't think it was as bad as it seems to be.'

'It should be clean, anyway. What does it feel like?'

'Right now, it's fine. When I walk and the muscle stretches it's hell.'

Their clothes were filthy, and no longer fit to use as bandages. Rorvik said, 'What about the offices? I might find something we can use.'

Baxter shuddered and shook his head. 'No thanks. It isn't as bad as that.'

They settled instead for cutting the edges of cloth back from the open wound; the searing beam of the igniter had closed off blood vessels as it passed, and the little blood that there was had begun to coagulate.

'I heard something going on down below,' Baxter said as Rorvik laboured to tear through the tough fabric.

'What do you mean?'

'Another part of the dome. A kind of rumble, and the walls shook. Didn't you hear it?'

'No.'

'I didn't imagine it. It was very distinct. A few minutes later there was another one, not quite as far away. I've an idea what it could be.'

'So have I. Somebody's followed us in and they're getting the same treatment. Fortunately we've a good start on them, and they'll never reach us in time. The chances are that Central will get them first with the new techniques it's learned, and once we've deprogrammed there's no going back.'

'What's to stop them from firing the programme up again?'

'It would have to be fed in step by step, and nobody can do that. It's taken Central over a hundred years to develop that programme, and it's all held in the memory underneath us. Cut the power and the molecules scatter.'

'And if they still come after us?'

'We'll worry about that when it happens. Did you see any robots on your way?'

'None. Did you?'

'No, but we'll stay alert anyway. We're not home yet.' Rorvik screwed up the remnant of cloth and threw it to one side.

'I can't see Central letting us in without a fight,' Baxter said doubtfully.

'Like it said, it's blind and its hands are tied. If it had the full use of its defences we'd never have gone farther than the door.'

Baxter was happy to concede the point. He held out his hand for Rorvik to help him up. It was at this moment that the steam pressure behind the corridor wall hit the crack point for the pipes. The blast was localised, but it was hard; it would be difficult to fault Central's timing. Rorvik found that he was holding the hand of a dead man.

There was comparative peace in the shaft as the dust settled, but Randall's ears were ringing. The protests of heated metal had been replaced by a steady drip of water down one wall from an unseen leak. He inadvertently reached through the falling drops and withdrew his hand sharply; they were hot, almost boiling.

Outside in the command centre Killoran heard a muttered exclamation and responded immediately, opening his microphone fader.

'Can you hear me?' he said. 'Are you all right?'

'Just about,' Randall's voice came back. 'Everything fell away from under me. I'm hanging onto the side, not too far from the top level. I'll climb the rigging and get out through the doors.'

'I've been trying to reach you. You weren't answering.'

There was badly-suppressed irritation in Randall's reply. 'If you'll forgive me, I had reason to be preoccupied. Besides which I couldn't hear anything over the noise here. I'm going to . . . ' There was a dull and distant thud, and the level of background static seemed to increase. Noise limiters cut in, and Randall's voice became softer and less distinct.

'That was something on the other side of the wall. It may have been intended for me, and if that's the case I'm not waiting to find out what.'

Randall began to haul himself upwards over the girders. Come on, he encouraged himself, you're Elite, tough and trained, you can out-think and outfight anything that moves. You're joking, his body protested. He managed to drag himself onto his belly on the next highest cross-piece and scramble to bring his legs up. After four such exercises he stopped to regain his breath and directed his light upward.

The top-level doors were only a little way above on the adjacent side. Beyond them the shadows of the gear at the top of the shaft were hung with stalactites of solidified metal and shrouded in steam.

After a short progress report he moved up to the doors and transferred over to their side. The footing here was less secure and most of his weight was out over the drop, so that only the grip of his hands prevented him from falling backwards.

There was no obvious way of opening the doors; no safety handle, no emergency switch. When he risked freeing one hand to attempt to prise them apart he found that they were locked solid.

Randall was on a nine-inch ledge and clinging to the bracing irons of the door frame. Above him was a suspended junkyard, below were four floors of precisely walled-in nothing. And the bloody doors wouldn't open, he added to complete the picture.

'Got a problem, chief?' Killoran asked tentatively.

'You might say so,' Randall replied bitterly. 'What does Tech know about elevator doors?'

There was an off-microphone conference. 'He says not much,' Killoran came back, 'but I'll put him on.'

There was more activity, and then Tech's voice came. He was leaning too close to the microphone.

'It's me, Randall,' he said. 'Have a look on the housing around the doors. See if you can find some sort of lever or wheel mechanism.'

Randall turned his body as far as he was able in order to direct the beam. The doorframe was surrounded by clusters of cables and junction boxes, and he began to describe them.

'No, you're looking for a lever,' Tech interrupted. 'It's one of those mechanical failsafe devices you were talking about before. The reason why the door won't open is that there's no car there to disengage the lock, so you'll have to do it manually.'

He saw it then, a sprung arm ending in a rubber wheel which projected from behind one of the guide rails. The top of an ascending car would raise it against the spring a few inches and disengage the deadlock on the outer doors. 'I think I've got it,' he reported, and then described the device.

'That sounds right. Try to lift it.'

First he had to reach it. He transferred back to the girderframe and moved up a couple of feet so that he wouldn't have to stretch too far and risk overbalancing. Even so he could only get his fingertips to the wheel, and it felt very solid. There was no give at all as he tried to press upwards, although his arm quivered with the effort.

'No good,' he told control. 'I can't get the leverage. It won't move at all.'

'I don't know what else I can suggest.'

'Don't worry about it. I'll see if I can shoot the lever off.'

Killoran came on the line, his voice urgent. 'Don't forget you've only got six charges.'

'They're no good to me in here, are they? And the longer I stay in one place the less chance I've got of escaping Central's notice.'

The blaster was a good, balanced fit in his hand. The weapons were powerful but inaccurate sidearms due to their fierce recoil, and as such were not standard issue, but he'd had his quota of practice on the Elite's ranges. The long-range hunting version had a damping mechanism which held the barrel level as the charge left it, but to have carried one of those monsters into Central would have been out of the question.

He flicked the safety switch into 'prime' mode, and waited a few seconds as a red light glowed. When it went out the weapon was live, and Randall wrapped his arm around the guide rail to absorb the recoil and then sighted on the centre of the lever.

Even at that range, he missed. His arm came up and away too soon, and the charge spent itself harmlessly in the brickwork and sent a bucketful of powder back over his head. The next shot hit, but off-centre. The lever bent and twisted, but in that way it only became more difficult to move. Randall gave it some time to cool, and reached over to see if he might have done any good. His fingertips flailed at the air a couple of inches short.

If the blaster shot so wide so close, what chance would he have with three running targets? That was, of course, assuming that the next charge freed the doors and left him with one shot per man. Damn Elite bureaucracy! If he'd co-operated fully he'd still be fighting with an oversized paper tag dangling from the handle.

He sighted again, this time reaching around the guide rail and holding his gun arm to steady it. He triggered the weapon, and the joints in his arm seemed to grind together from the recoil as the plug of charged particles sped from the barrel and buried their energy in the metal rod only two feet away.

It burst apart along the lines of stress determined by the previous impact, and the entire mechanism fell away and rattled off down the shaft. The spring was left hanging loose, so that Randall had either disengaged the doors or sealed them completely. He de-primed and replaced the blaster on his belt, and then made his way back to the narrow ledge. Balancing himself with one hand he tried with the other to prise the doors apart at the point where their surfaces curved slightly and met.

Too hard, and his fingernails scraped and tore on the metal as they skidded across. This time he used a more gentle pressure, and felt springs reluctantly begin to give; then there was a crack enough to reach his hand into, and his arm was through before the double doors could ease together again. A hard thrust of his shoulder and they both retracted fully whilst his momentum carried him on and out into the top-level corridor.

Behind him the doors closed soundlessly. He was in a corridor strewn with rubble and filled with steam, and it reflected his glow like a fog. Randall realised that Killoran was talking to him, and began to answer. His assistant seemed not to hear, and Randall put his hand to his collar microphone to find that its connecting lead had been pulled loose. He found the dangling plug and inserted it into the small socket stitched into the shoulder padding. Then he answered again.

'What's happening up there?' Killoran said as soon as he realised that Randall was back in communication. 'We heard two shots and then lost the signal altogether.'

'Loose wire. I'm as high as I can go, and the place is a mess. Half the ceiling's come down and the plumbing's ruptured.'

'Rorvik's work?'

'I don't see how. You want to see it up here. More likely it's Central's work as part of the reprogramming; anybody standing alongside wouldn't have much of a chance.'

'Keep us informed.'

Randall was about to protest, then realised that a delay now for his own comfort was out of the question. The raiding party were somewhere near, and this wasn't the time for recuperation. Suppressing the giddiness of relief he arose and stepped over the rubble into the fog.

He tripped within seconds, and as he fell his outstretched hand carried his full weight onto something soft and warm. There was a terrifying, inhuman groan, and Randall withdrew his hand immediately; then, more tentatively, he reached out and probed amongst the dust and swirling vapour.

It was a body, and a few seconds' investigation showed it to be no longer alive. Randall had driven the air from its dead lungs and given it a momentary semblance of animation. He turned it over with difficulty and brushed the sticky paste of plaster dust and condensation off its features. He could tell it was a citizen, but was it Rorvik?

Not this time. As Randall lifted the head towards his beam he knew that it wasn't the face he'd studied and searched for since the disastrous Grade Two so long ago.

It must be Baxter, then. He let the head with its half-open eyes drop back, and his hand came away purple and wet. He hardly noticed, wiping the mess absently on his jacket as he studied the dusty floor for footprints. The steam swirled and cleared a little and he shook drops of dew from his eyebrows. His clothes were sticky with the humidity.

Only one trail led away, with no sign of the third man. Central had so far scored two out of four, but time was now short; unclipping the blaster again Randall stepped over the dead man and followed the footprints.

They petered out after a few yards, and he was left only with a general direction. Feeling the growing desperation of a rat in a maze as the scent of comfort grows even fainter he began to check the corridors which angled away. At first he gave each little more than a glance, but as the blind alleys and wrong turnings accumulated he found that he had to return to look again and be sure. Randall knew that he had to follow a general direction inward from the curve of the main passage but had no other guide; and all these passageways looked the same. He couldn't be sure that he wasn't wandering through the same ones over and over again.

Only the main corridor was recognisable, being wider than the others and having no abrupt turns in its gentle sweep. He would have to adopt some kind of system of search, and use this as his main reference point. Only when he came to scrape a mark on the next corner did he realise that somebody else had used the same idea.

It was a numeral, barely legible, and it had been struck out with a cross. The next junction was the same, and the next one after that. Two more and – but an uneasy thought sent him back to the last symbol to look again.

What he had hastily read as a striking-out was no such thing. It was a crude line dragged under the numeral, and an exclamation mark after it.

Rorvik and Baxter had been searching separately. One or the other found success, and they had met again in the corridor near the elevator, where Central had waited and managed to swat one of them. The fate of the third man was as obscure as his origins, but only Rorvik was ahead now.

At the sight of the unhooked door and the open area beyond Randall paused to douse the beam that would betray his presence.

'I've arrived, Neil,' he reported in a whisper. 'Don't transmit to me in case Rorvik hears anything - overspill from the earpiece or something like that.'

'Shouldn't be any danger of it, but I'll keep the fader down at this end anyway. I don't want to distract you.'

Randall's eyes adjusted to the overall glow that seeped into the corridor, and after a moment he stepped through the open doorway.

It was quiet, most unlike the raucous computer room in the Elite building. This was indeed the apex of the dome, for its top curved overhead, the broken panes of panelling seen through a bracing framework. He was screened from the rest of the circular chamber by a series of wedges of electronics banks taller and wider than himself, stacked in rows and separated by narrow avenues all of which arrowed in towards the chamber's centre.

There was a rustle, and then the definite sound of metal against metal somewhere over towards that centre. Randall slipped sideways into the nearest avenue and edged silently down it.

Rorvik crouched by the operator's console, a fixed semicircular desk which was surfaced with an array of coloured lights and three prominent keys. He was reaching into a small pouch, and withdrew an object that Randall recognised. It was the right-handed partner to the insulated glove found in the underbelly.

He pulled it on and worked his fingers into it as he crossed to the inner curve of panelling on the electronics banks opposite Randall. The panels hinged open easily, and revealed nothing of much wonder or surprise; ordered stacks of silvery printed wafers, hundreds of them edge-on. Wire and glass linked and cross-linked the layers.

Rorvik was looking into the open casing. The glove was obviously intended to smash and rip, and Randall knew that he shouldn't be letting Rorvik so close to the edge; but in his mind, it was Randall himself who stood ready to destroy, Randall himself who was picking his place and gathering all the accumulated frustrations of his life, Randall himself drawn to the desert mirage of a better life without Central.

Rorvik broke the spell. He pulled off the glove, and dropped it.

Randall saw his face as he turned. He didn't see the face that he was expecting, the tense, dangerous man that brought down 'copters and danced easily beyond reach; he saw only a citizen, frightened and broken, too weak to finish what he started.

The disappointment was solid and physical; it had a bitter taste, and it screwed Randall up deep down inside. *You can't do this to me,* he thought, *you can't bring me so close and then back off.* Rorvik was wiping his eyes on his sleeve, a soft-toy version of a hero. Randall stepped from hiding and raised the blaster.

As Rorvik's arm came down he saw the Elite, and his eyes widened. His skin, hair and clothes were dust-white and flecked with Baxter's blood. Randall was a contrast in the soot and grease of the elevator shaft, more of Baxter's blood on his side; Baxter made them brothers, touched the opposites and pulled them together.

All around them, the clean song of the machine continued. The soft and vulnerable parts of Central ticked on without obvious concern. Rorvik swallowed hard and raised his hands.

It was too much for Randall; it made a joke of the scenario. He shot Rorvik twice.

The first shot threw him back into the open circuitry, the second caught him as he bounced out and spun him around. He hit the floor with a heavy, no-life sound, mangled up and twisted by the charges. He lay still.

There was an ache in Randall's wrist as he crossed the central open area and looked down at the body; no need to check for life, Rorvik was half blown apart. There was some localised damage in the machine stacks behind him, snow crystals that gritted underfoot. Rorvik was dead not for what he'd done, but for what he'd failed to do; the price in lives and effort didn't allow any backing-off at the end. Randall had been following an opponent, a respectable fantasy, and Rorvik hadn't been big enough to fill out the shape; so who was going to fill it out now?

The microphone lead at his shoulder had come adrift again. He reconnected it. 'Rorvik's dead, Neil,' he said.

'Well done. We lost you again for a while.'

'I know. Accident.' Aware that he was avoiding looking directly across to the operator's console, Randall stepped around Rorvik to where the belt-pouch lay open on the floor. Central hummed gently on all sides.

First to come out of the pouch were three crudely-shaped probes and 'drivers. The tip of one of them was burnt blue, and Randall dropped them on one side. The only other object was a plain box with a hinged lid.

Randall opened it carefully, expecting to find explosives. As the lid came open he heard the starting whirr of a motor – the damn thing was a booby-trap! He threw it away and dived behind the console.

It bounced once, twice, and Randall covered his head with his arms. The box rolled and came to a stop with its lid open, and the motor continued to turn.

Randall unfroze, and pushed himself sheepishly to his knees. Then he stood up and went around the console to where the musical box was playing.

'What's going on now?' The microphone was picking

up the signal. After a few bars the tune began to repeat.

'Nothing,' Randall said, and disconnected the microphone lead.

Collinson was twiddling the tuning dial on his ancient receiver when a light began to flash on his switchboard. Mumbling to himself in irritation he turned off the power and went over to answer the call.

'What is it?' he demanded, making no effort to conceal his mood.

He recognised the replying voice immediately; Gerrard, old man on the fourth floor. He rarely came out and almost never made requests, but now he was saying, 'It's my public broadcast speaker. I wonder if you could have a look at it for me?'

'I don't know. I've got a lot on.' If pressed for a justification, no doubt Collinson would think of something.

'When you've finished, then? I don't want to be any trouble.'

'All right, when I've finished.'

Collinson hung up and returned to his receiver. With the power on everything seemed to be working, but the wavebands just hissed with static. He would have to have it repaired, and then find some way of losing the bill in the apartment block's accounts.

He switched the set off in disgust, and dropped into his armchair. It wheezed as air bled out of all its seams under his weight, but he couldn't feel comfortable; the silence in the glassed-in office disturbed him. Outside, the building's lobby was quiet, but the faint and random sounds of the street beyond drifted in and settled like dust around him.

With a sigh of irritation he opened a drawer and took out a sheaf of official requisition forms and billings for citizens' property from Central Command. He stuffed them untidily under the sprung jaws on his clipboard and went out to call the elevator.

It rumbled down from the fifth floor. Collinson feigned an amiable greeting to the citizen woman that emerged, and then pulled the double doors behind him and pressed the fourth floor button. The recently-repaired mechanism jerked a couple of times and then began to haul the car upwards.

Gerrard followed him from the door and watched anxiously as he looked over the set. Collinson was aware that he had no technical knowledge or ability, but Gerrard didn't know that and so he turned all the dials and altered all the settings and nodded knowingly at each result. In the end he gave his verdict.

'It's not working,' he said.

'It's not switched on,' Gerrard pointed out.

'I know that,' Collinson said quickly. 'These are tests we do *before* it's switched on. You can learn a lot that way.'

Gerrard seemed suitably impressed, and Collinson tried again with the power on. After a few seconds he paused, uncertain; the set's speaker was hissing with the same formless static as his own.

'It went off suddenly, about ten minutes ago,' Gerrard said.

Collinson's switchboard was unattended, four floors down. There was an indicator which corresponded to each of the citizens' apartments in the block. One by one, they started to come alight.

THE HUMANOID TOUCH

Jack Williamson
author of THE HUMANOIDS

More than thirty years ago Jack Williamson created one of the finest science fiction novels of all time – THE HUMANOIDS. In this new novel he returns to his classic subject: the final confrontation of man and machine. THE HUMANOID TOUCH is a new peak for a master of science fiction.

'Decades before the current headlines about automaton, computers and robots, Jack Williamson was examining the relationship between humankind and machines in his stories of the Humanoids. Now, in THE HUMANOID TOUCH, the Grand Master of Science Fiction carries that saga to its final, irresistible step. This is science fiction at its best: thoughtful, thought-provoking, and thoroughly engrossing.' *Ben Bova*

SCIENCE FICTION 0 7221 9195 2 £1.75

BEYOND GENESIS, BEYOND 2001 .

MISSION

PATRICK TILLEY

Easter Saturday. The naked body of a 35 year old man is rushed to Manhattan General Hospital. He has a two-inch stab wound below his rib-cage and nail wounds in his feet and wrists. The impossible has happened: Jesus Christ has appeared 7000 miles and 20 centuries away from the Crucifixion – dead on arrival.

What can the witnesses do? What would *you* do?

MISSION is powerful and compelling fiction by Patrick Tilley, author of FADE-OUT. It is also a stunning reassessment of the central truths and deepest beliefs by which we live.

'Extraordinary, original . . . has all the makings of a huge success . . . a word-of-mouth cult book . . . I urge you to read it.' *Sunday Express*

GENERAL FICTION 0 7221 0504 5 £1.95

TIME SCAPE

Winner of the 1981 Nebula Award

GREGORY BENFORD

The year is 1998, the world is a growing nightmare of desperation, of uncontrollable pollution and increasing social unrest.

In Cambridge, two scientists experiment with tachyons – subatomic particles that travel faster than the speed of light and, therefore, according to the Theory of Relativity, may move backwards in time. Their plan is to signal a warning to the previous generation . . .

In 1962, a young Californian scientist, Gordon Bernstein, finds his experiments are being spoiled by unknown interference. As he begins to suspect something near the truth it becomes a race against time – the world is collapsing and will only be saved if Gordon can decipher the messages in time.

GENERAL FICTION 0 7221 1630 6 £1.75

the trade

william h. hallahan

'Puts William Hallahan up above Le Carré, Deighton and Co.'
The Bookseller

Journalist Bernie Parker didn't make a lot of sense that day. His words needed a bit of explanation. But Bernie is in no position to do that right now because he's just stopped several bullets outside a Paris metro. Bernie is dead. And no one knows what his last words mean.

The least Colin Thomas owes his late friend is a reason. As an international arms dealer scoring off the hotter edges of the cold war he has contacts. Contacts that lead him back to a ruthless and uninhibited woman and to the centre of a devastating plan to change the face of Europe – even if it means starting World War 3 – even if it means starting the countdown to doomsday . . .

ADVENTURE THRILLER 0 7221 4215 3 £1.75